"GOING OUT OF BUSINESS"

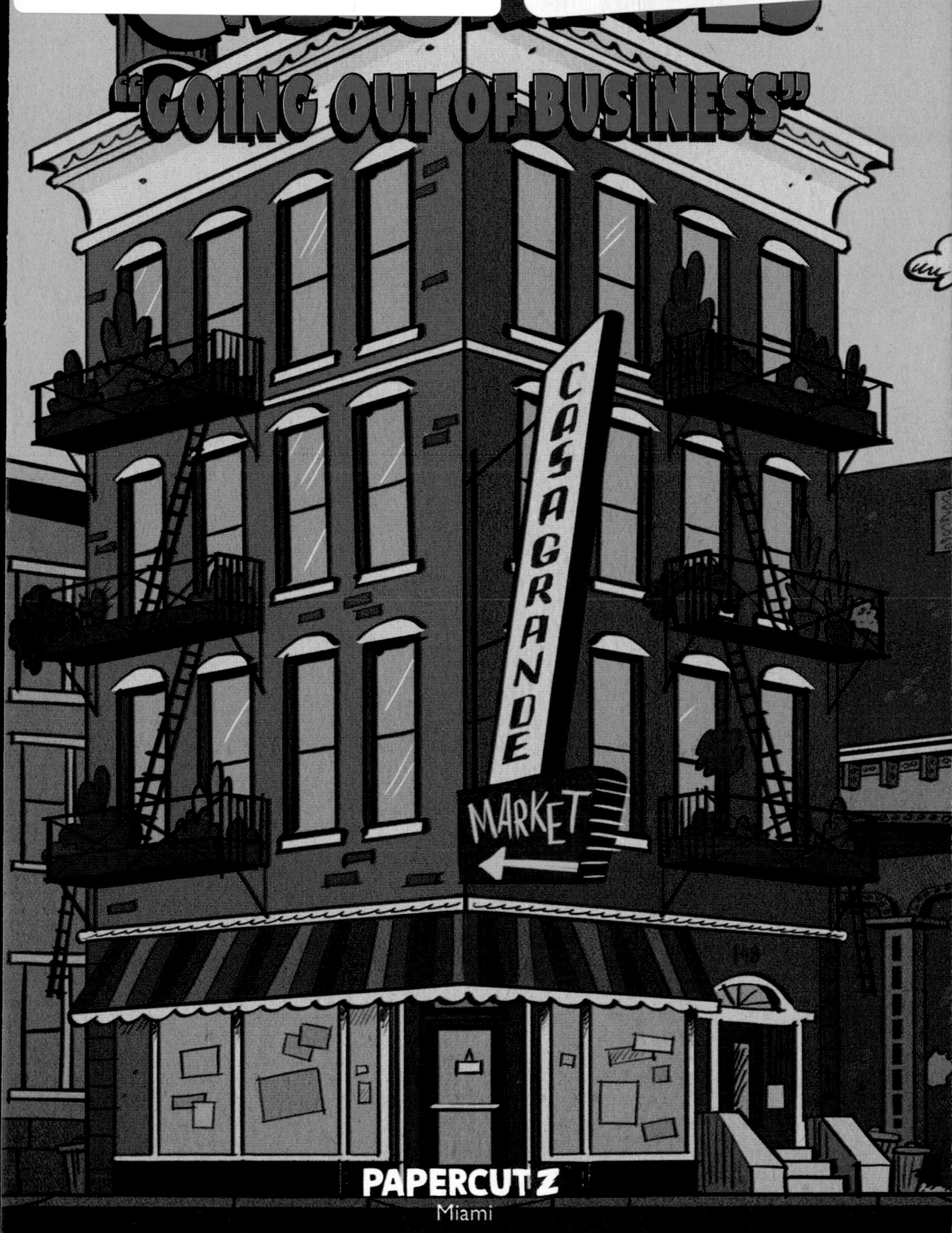
CASAGRANDE
MARKET

PAPERCUTZ
Miami

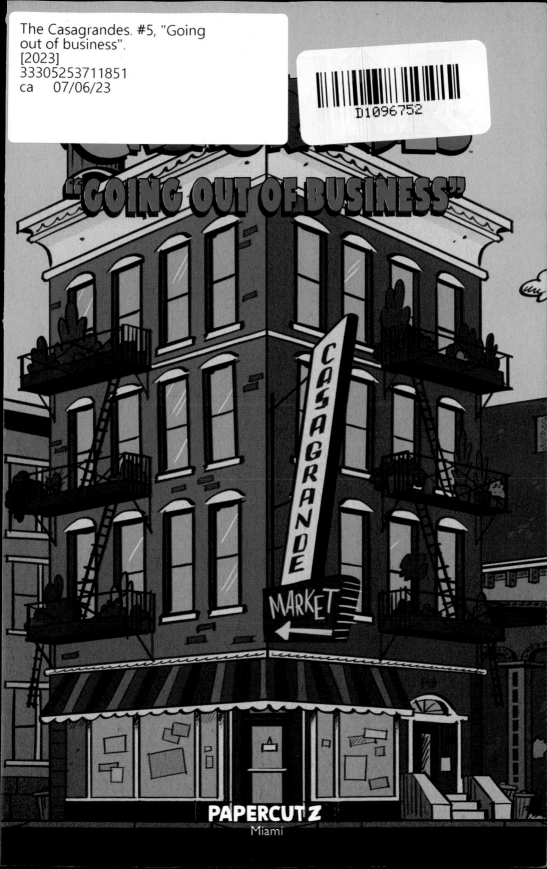

MORE GREAT GRAPHIC NOVEL SERIES AVAILABLE FROM

PAPERCUTZ™

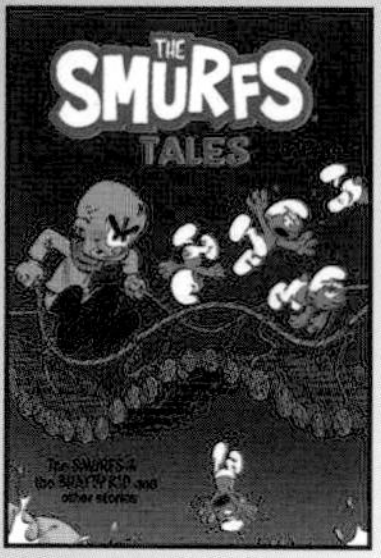
THE SMURFS
TALES
PAPERCUTZ
THE SMURFS TALES

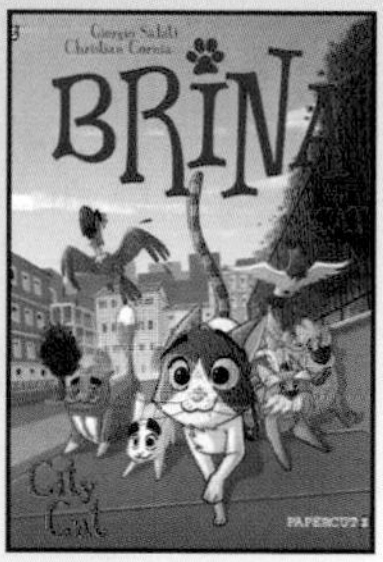
BRINA
City Cat
PAPERCUTZ
BRINA THE CAT

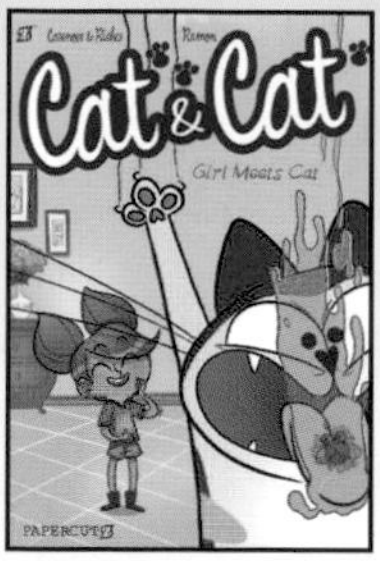
Cat & Cat
Girl Meets Cat
PAPERCUTZ
CAT & CAT

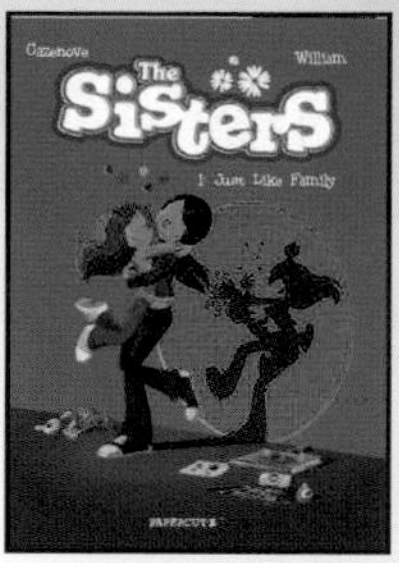
The Sisters
1 Just Like Family
PAPERCUTZ
THE SISTERS

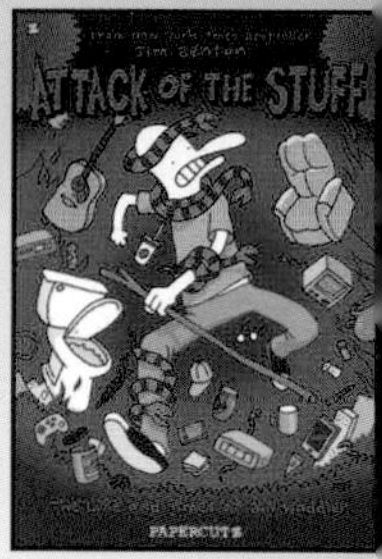
ATTACK OF THE STUFF
PAPERCUTZ
ATTACK OF THE STUFF

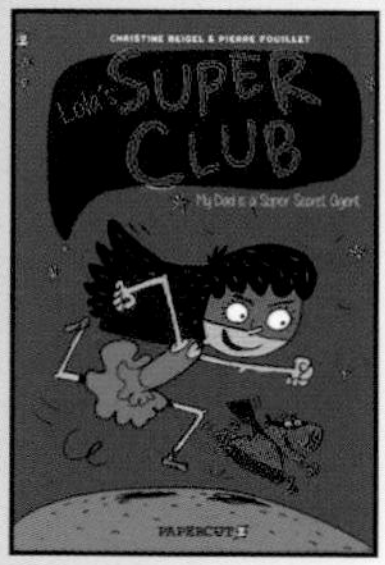
CHRISTINE BEIGEL & PIERRE FOUILLET
Lola's SUPER CLUB
PAPERCUTZ
LOLA'S SUPER CLUB

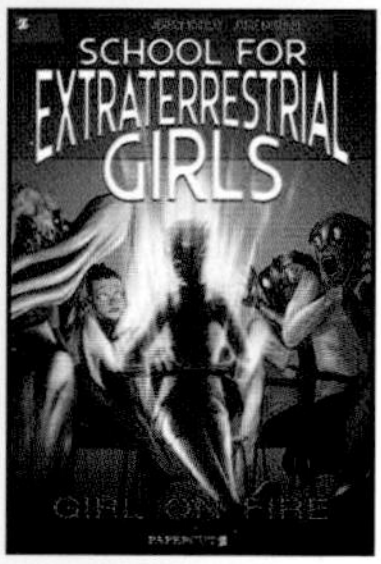
SCHOOL FOR EXTRATERRESTRIAL GIRLS
GIRL ON FIRE
PAPERCUTZ
SCHOOL FOR EXTRATERRESTRIAL GIRLS

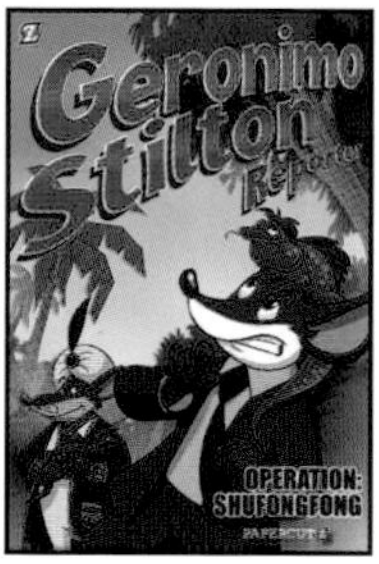
Geronimo Stilton Reporter
OPERATION: SHUFONGFONG
PAPERCUTZ
GERONIMO STILTON REPORTER

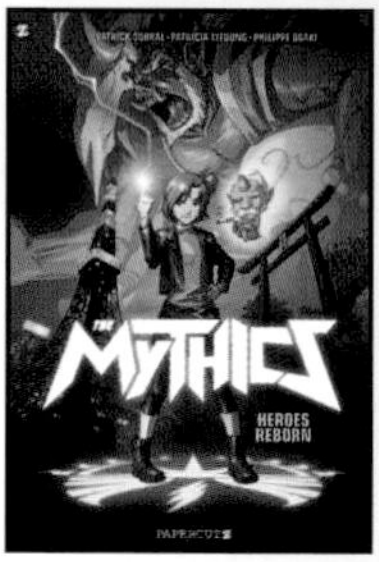
THE MYTHICS
HEROES REBORN
PAPERCUTZ
THE MYTHICS

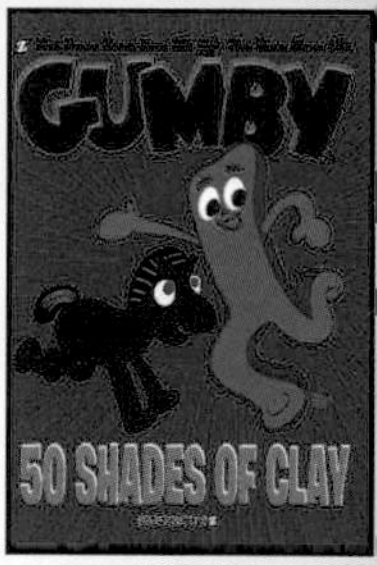
GUMBY
50 SHADES OF CLAY
PAPERCUTZ
GUMBY

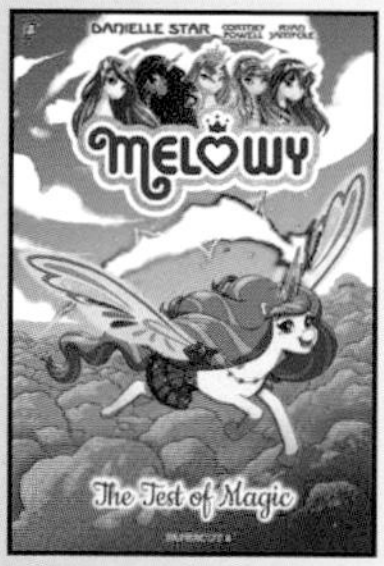
DANIELLE STAR
MELOWY
The Test of Magic
PAPERCUTZ
MELOWY

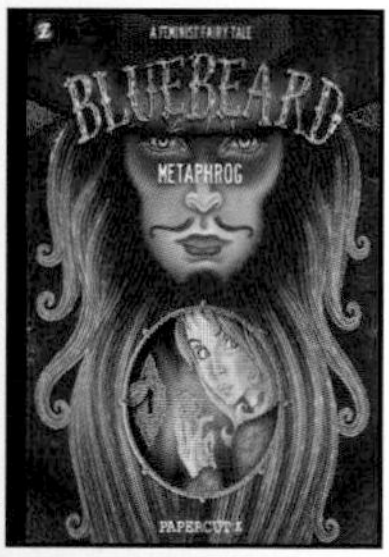
A FEMINIST FAIRY TALE
BLUEBEARD
METAPHROG
PAPERCUTZ
BLUEBEARD

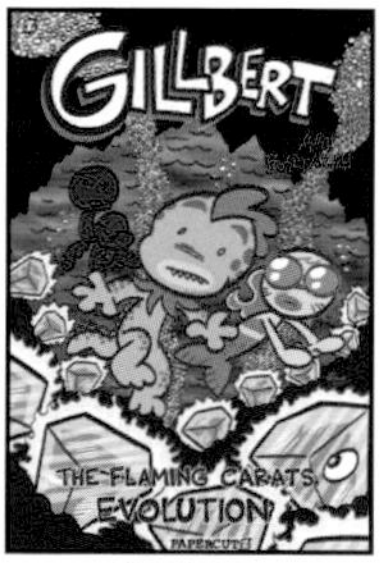
GILLBERT
THE FLAMING CARATS EVOLUTION
PAPERCUTZ
GILLBERT

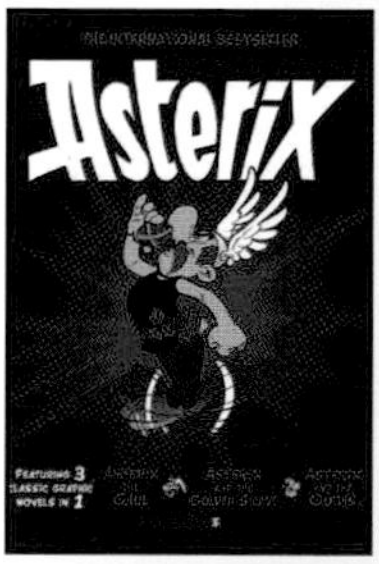
Asterix
FEATURING 3 CLASSIC GRAPHIC NOVELS IN 1
ASTERIX

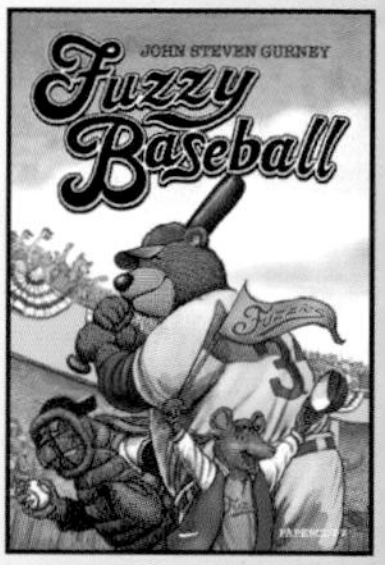
JOHN STEVEN GURNEY
Fuzzy Baseball
PAPERCUTZ
FUZZY BASEBALL

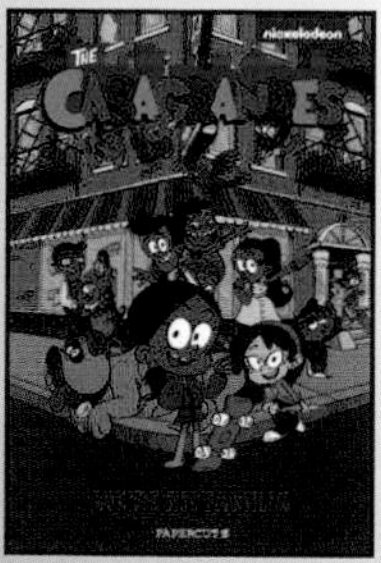
nickelodeon
THE CASAGRANDES
PAPERCUTZ
THE CASAGRANDES

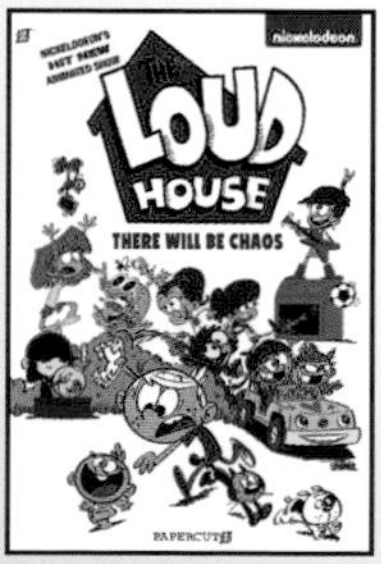
nickelodeon
THE LOUD HOUSE
THERE WILL BE CHAOS
PAPERCUTZ
THE LOUD HOUSE

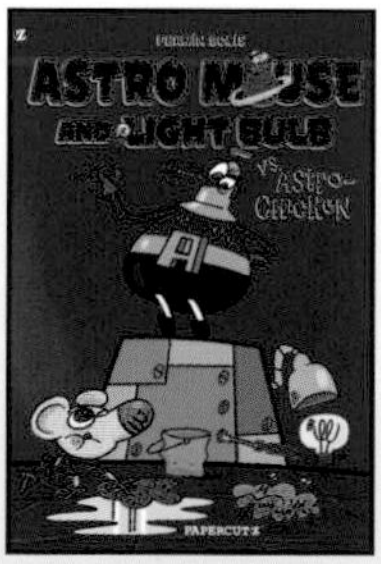
ASTRO MOUSE AND LIGHT BULB
PAPERCUTZ
ASTRO MOUSE AND LIGHT BULB

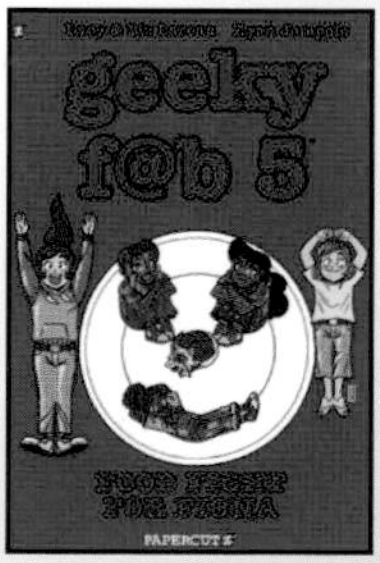
geeky f@b 5
PAPERCUTZ
GEEKY F@B 5

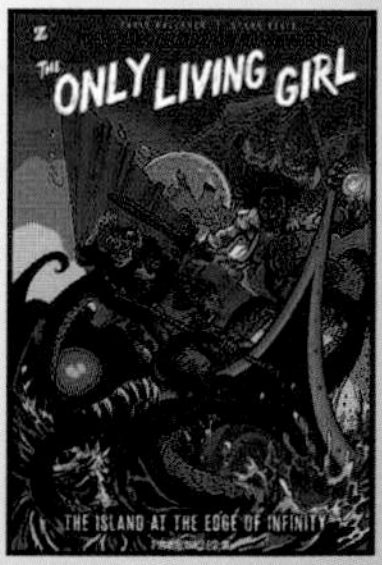
THE ONLY LIVING GIRL
THE ISLAND AT THE EDGE OF INFINITY
THE ONLY LIVING GIRL

papercutz.com

Also available where ebooks are sold.

THE CASAGRANDES

#5 "GOING OUT OF BUSINESS"

nickelodeon THE CASAGRANDES #5 "GOING OUT OF BUSINESS"

"EL FAL-CON"
Erik Steinman — Writer
Amanda Tran — Artist, Colorist
Bryan Senka — Letterer

"MARIACHI MIGUEL"
Jair Holguin — Writer
Gabi Ayala — Artist, Colorist
Bryan Senka — Letterer

"BEAR WITH IT"
Derek Fridolfs — Writer
Ida Denney — Artist
Erin Rodriguez — Colorist
Bryan Senka — Letterer

"NIGHT MERCADO"
Jay Choi — Writer
Amanda Tran — Artist, Colorist
Bryan Senka — Letterer

"THE DOCTOR IS IN"
Mikey Lewis — Writer
Lex Moisson — Artist, Colorist
Bryan Senka — Letterer

"ALONE TIME"

"BABY MAKES BANK"
Erik Steinman — Writer
Izzy Boyce-Blanchard — Artist, Colorist
Bryan Senka — Letterer

AMANDA TRAN — Color Artist
JAMES SALERNO — Sr. Art Director/Nickelodeon
JAYJAY JACKSON — Design

ISBN: 978-1-5458-1048-4 paperback edition
ISBN: 978-1-5458-1047-7 hardcover edition

Published by Mad Cave Studios and Papercutz.
www.papercutz.com

Printed in China
June 2023

First Printing

THE CASAGRANDES

Theme Song Performed by: ALLY BROOKE
Theme Song Composed by: GERMAINE FRANCO
Lyrics by: GERMAINE FRANCO, MIKE RUBINER & LALO ALCARAZ
Rap Lyrics Performed by: IZABELLA ALVAREZ

I'm in the big city with my big familia [family]

Everyday here is my favorite día [day]

One big house and our family store
Food and laughter ¡y mucho amor! [and a lot of love!]

Tíos [aunts and uncles], abuelos [grandparents], all of my primos [cousins]...

A dog, a parrot, amigos! [friends!]

We're one big family now!
Sundays and Mondays
They're all fun days when you're with the...
Casagrandes!
¡Mucha vida! [A lot of life!]

Casagrandes!
¡Bienvenida! [Welcome!]

Casagrandes!
¡Mucha risa! [A lot of laughs!]

Casagrandes!
We're all familia! [Family!]

¡Tan-tan! [Tah-dah!]

MEET THE CASAGRANDES
and friends!

RONNIE ANNE SANTIAGO

Ronnie Anne's a skateboarding city girl now. She's fearless, free-spirited, and always quick to come up with a plan. She's one tough cookie, but she also has a sweet side. Ronnie Anne loves helping her family, and that's taught her to help others too. When she's not pitching in at the family *mercado*, you can find her exploring the neighborhood with her best friend Sid, or ordering hot dogs with her skater buds Casey, Nikki, and Sameer. Having a family as big as the Casagrandes has taught Ronnie Anne to deal with anything life throws her way.

BOBBY SANTIAGO

Bobby is Ronnie Anne's big bro. He's a student and one of the hardest workers in the city. He loves his family and loves working at the *mercado*. As his *abuelo's* right hand man, Bobby can't wait to take over the family business one day. He's a big kid at heart, and his clumsiness gets him into some sticky situations at work, like locking himself in the freezer. *Mercado* mishaps aside, everyone in the neighborhood loves to come to the store and talk to Bobby.

MARIA CASAGRANDE SANTIAGO

Maria is Bobby and Ronnie Anne's mom. As a nurse at the city hospital, she's hardworking and even harder to gross out. For years, Maria, Bobby, and Ronnie Anne were used to only having each other… but now that they've moved in with their Casagrande relatives, they're embracing big family life. Maria is the voice of reason in the household and known for her always-on-the-go attitude. Her long work hours means she doesn't always get to spend time with Bobby and Ronnie Anne; but when she does, she makes that time count.

HECTOR CASAGRANDE

Hector is Carlos and Maria's dad, and the *abuelo* of the family (that means grandpa)! He owns the *mercado* on the ground floor of their apartment building and takes great pride in his work, his family, and being the unofficial "mayor" of the block. He loves to tell stories, share his ideas, and gossip (even though he won't admit to it). You can find him working in the *mercado*, playing guitar, or watching his favorite *telenovela*.

ROSA CASAGRANDE

Rosa is Carlos and Maria's mom and the *abuela* of the family (that means grandma)! She's the head of the household, the wisest Casagrande, and the master cook with a superhuman ability to tell when anyone in the house is hungry. She often tries to fix problems or illnesses with traditional Mexican home remedies and potions. She's very protective of her family… sometimes a little too much.

CARLOS CASAGRANDE

Carlos is Maria's brother. He's married to Frida, and together they have four kids: Carlota, C.J., Carl, and Carlitos. Carlos is a Professor of Cultural Studies at a local college. Usually he has his head in the clouds or his nose in a textbook. Relatively easygoing, Carlos is a loving father and an enthusiastic teacher who tries to get his kids interested in their Mexican heritage.

FRIDA PUGA CASAGRANDE

Frida is Carlota, C.J., Carl, and Carlitos' mom. She's an art professor and a performance artist, and is always looking for new ways to express herself. She's got a big heart and isn't shy about her emotions. Frida tends to cry when she's sad, happy, angry, or any other emotion you can think of. She's always up for fun, is passionate about her art, and loves her family more than anything.

CARLOTA CASAGRANDE

Carlota is CJ, Carl, and Carlitos' older sister. A social media influencer, she's excited to be like a big sister to Ronnie Anne. She's a force to be reckoned with, and is always trying to share her distinctive vintage style tips with Ronnie Anne.

CARLITOS CASAGRANDE

Carlitos is the baby of the family, and is always copying the behavior of everyone in the household—even if they aren't human. He's a playful and silly baby who loves to play with the family pets.

CJ (CARLOS JR.) CASAGRANDE

CJ is Carlota's younger brother and Carl and Carlitos' older brother. He was born with Down Syndrome. He lights up any room with his infectious smile and is always ready to play. He's obsessed with pirates and is BFFs with Bobby. He likes to wear a bowtie to any family occasion, and you can always catch him laughing or helping his *abuela*.

CARL CASAGRANDE

Carl is wise beyond his years. He's confident, outgoing, and puts a lot of time and effort into looking good. He likes to think of himself as a suave businessman and doesn't like to get caught playing with his action figures or wearing his footie PJs. Even though Bobby is nothing but nice to him, Carl sees his big cousin as his biggest rival.

LALO

Lalo is a slobbery bull mastiff who thinks he's a lapdog. He's not the smartest pup, and gets scared easily… but he loves his family and loves to cuddle.

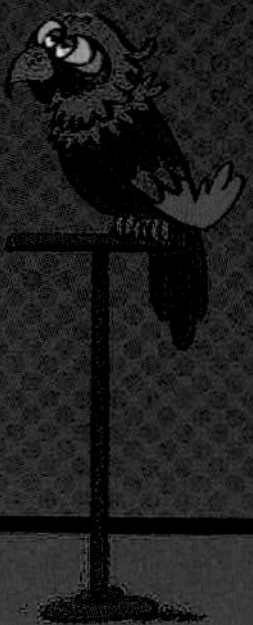

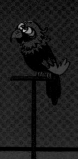

SERGIO

Sergio is the Casagrandes' beloved pet parrot. He's a blunt, sassy bird who "thinks" he's full of wisdom and always has something to say. The Casagrandes have to keep a close eye on their credit card as Sergio is addicted to online shopping and is always asking the family to buy him some new gadget he saw on TV. Sergio is most loyal to Rosa and serves as her wing-man, partner-in-crime, taste-tester, and confidant. Sergio is quite popular in the neighborhood and is always up for a good time. When he's not working part time at the *mercado* (aka messing with Bobby), he can be found hanging with his roommate Ronnie Anne, partying with Sancho and his other pigeon pals, or trying to get his ex-girlfriend, Priscilla (an ostrich at the zoo), to respond to him.

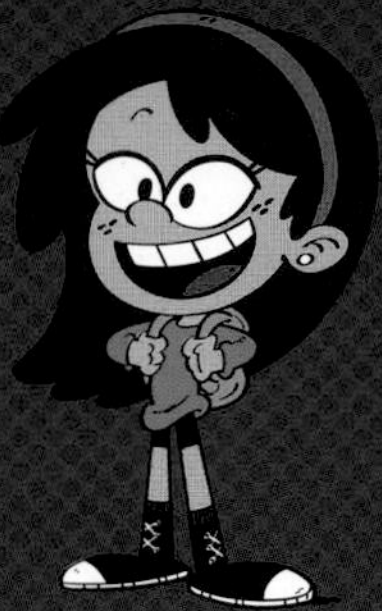

SID CHANG

Sid is Ronnie Anne's quirky best friend. She's new to the city but dives headfirst into everything she finds interesting. She and her family just moved into the apartment one floor above the Casagrandes. In fact, Sid's bedroom is right above Ronnie Anne's. A dream come true for any BFFs.

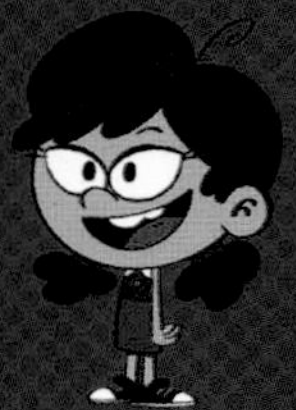

ADELAIDE CHANG

Adelaide Chang is Sid's little sister. She's 6 years old, and has a flair for the dramatic. You can always find her trying to make her way into her big sister Sid's adventures.

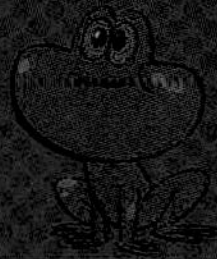

FROGGY 2

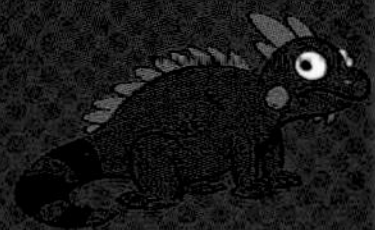

MEATBALL

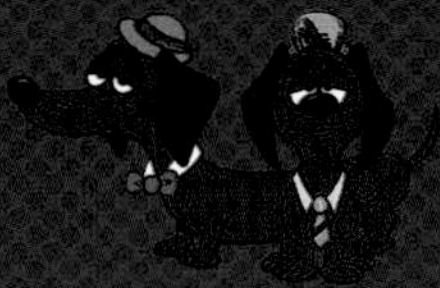

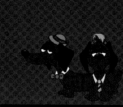

BIG TONY & LITTLE SAL

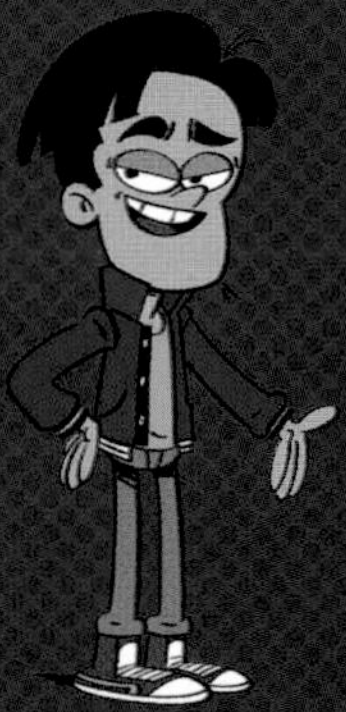

CORY NAKAMURA

Cory is the teenaged son of Mr. Nakamura. He likes playing video games and hanging out at the *Mercado* late when he has insomnia.

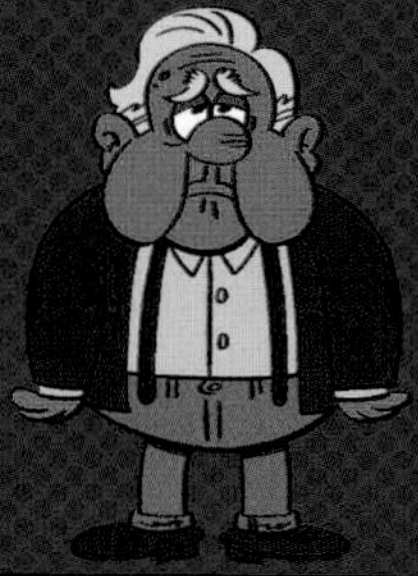

VITO FILLIPONIO

Vito is one of Rosa and Hector's oldest and dearest friends, and a frequent customer at the Mercado. He's lovable, nosy, and usually overstays his welcome, but there is nothing he wouldn't do for his loved ones and his dogs, Big Tony and Little Sal.

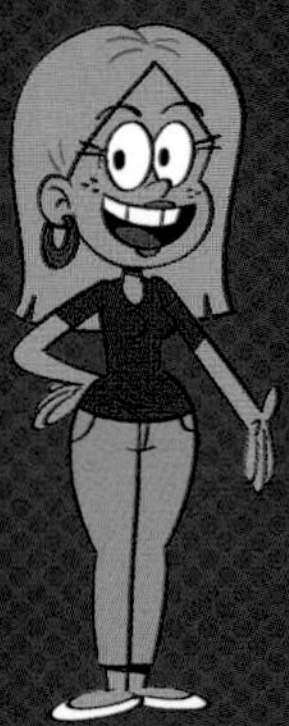

BECCA CHANG

Becca Chang is Sid's mom. Like her daughter, Becca is quirky, smart, and funny. She works at the Great Lakes City Zoo and often brings her work home with her, which means the Chang household can also be a bit of a zoo!

PHILLIP "FLIP" PHILLIPINI

Flip is the owner of Flip's Food and Fuel, the local convenience store. Flip has questionable business practices; he's been known to sell expired milk and soak his feet in the nacho cheese! Flip's a tough businessman; there's nothing he wouldn't do to save a buck. Flip also goes by several aliases, all of whom also operate odd businesses in Royal Woods: Tony, of Tony's Tows N Toes, Tucker of Tucker's Tix N Tux, and Pat of Pat's Prawn N' Pawn's, etc. Flip's got a huge soft spot for the high school gal that got away, turkey mogul Tammy Gobblesworth, and is tickled to have rekindled a relationship with her now.

LORI LOUD

As the first-born child of the Loud Clan, Lori sees herself as the boss of all her siblings. She feels she's paved the way for them and deserves extra respect. Her signature traits are rolling her eyes, texting her boyfriend, Bobby, and literally saying "literally" all the time. Because she's the oldest and most experienced sibling, Lori can be a great ally, so it pays to stay on her good side, especially since she can drive.

PAR

Par is the *Mercado's* produce delivery guy. He's an outgoing, thrill-seeking dude with a deep appreciation for quality fruits and vegetables. He loves hanging out with his pal Bobby and if you're ever looking for a fun time filled with adventure, definitely call the Par-Dawg!

NELSON

NACHO

Flip's Best Friend

ERNESTO ESTRELLA

Ernesto is a seasoned astrologer appearing on very theatrical television segments to give advice and make daily predictions based on his reading of the stars. *Abuela* Rosa has been Ernesto's biggest fan ever since he started foretelling the future, decades ago. This all-knowing, flamboyant mystic has a flare for the magical and the dramatic, dressing in very elaborate, curated looks. He is a Puerto Rican who speaks lightly accented English and of course fluent, and florid Spanish. Ernesto pops in and out of the Casagrande's world (on TV and in their minds) weighing in on *"tu destino!"* Ernesto Estrella may be in his late 60s, but one can only guess as Ernesto tells the future, not his age.

MR. NAKAMURA

"EL FAL-CON"

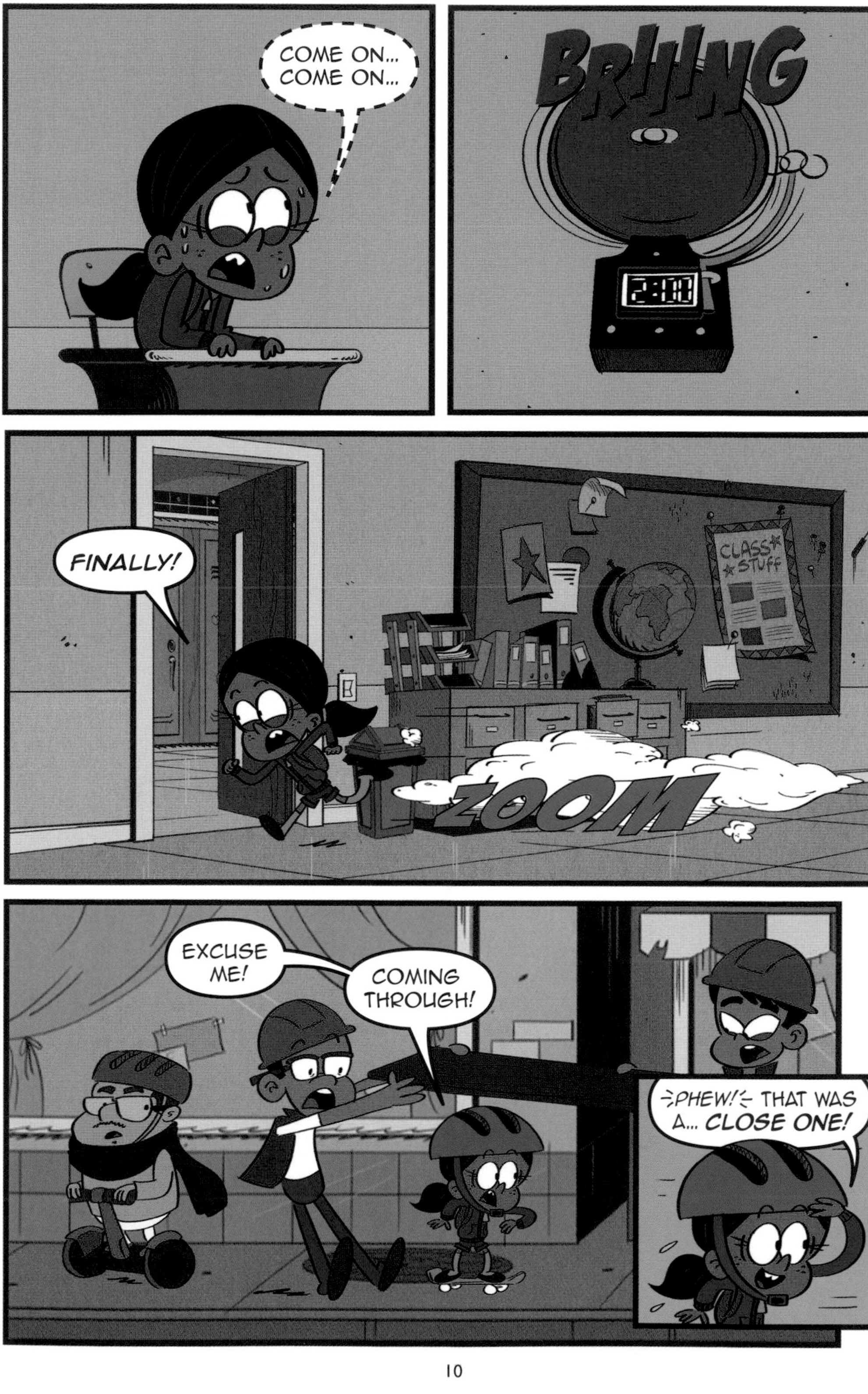
COME ON... COME ON...
BRIIING
2:00
FINALLY!
CLASS STUFF
ZOOM
EXCUSE ME!
COMING THROUGH!
PHEW! THAT WAS A... CLOSE ONE!

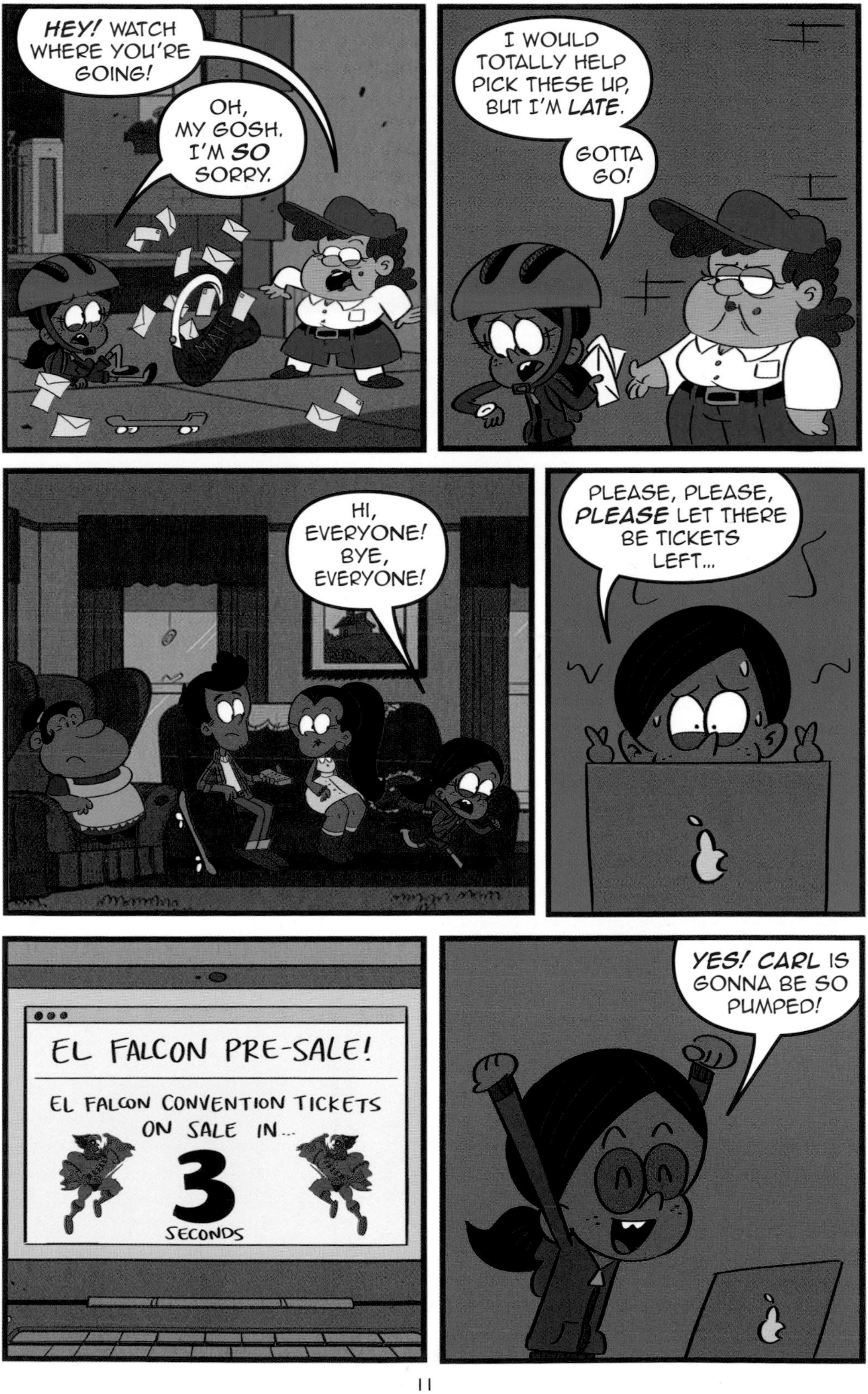
HEY! WATCH WHERE YOU'RE GOING!
OH, MY GOSH. I'M SO SORRY.
I WOULD TOTALLY HELP PICK THESE UP, BUT I'M LATE.
GOTTA GO!
HI, EVERYONE! BYE, EVERYONE!
PLEASE, PLEASE, PLEASE LET THERE BE TICKETS LEFT...
EL FALCON PRE-SALE!
EL FALCON CONVENTION TICKETS ON SALE IN...
3
SECONDS
YES! CARL IS GONNA BE SO PUMPED!

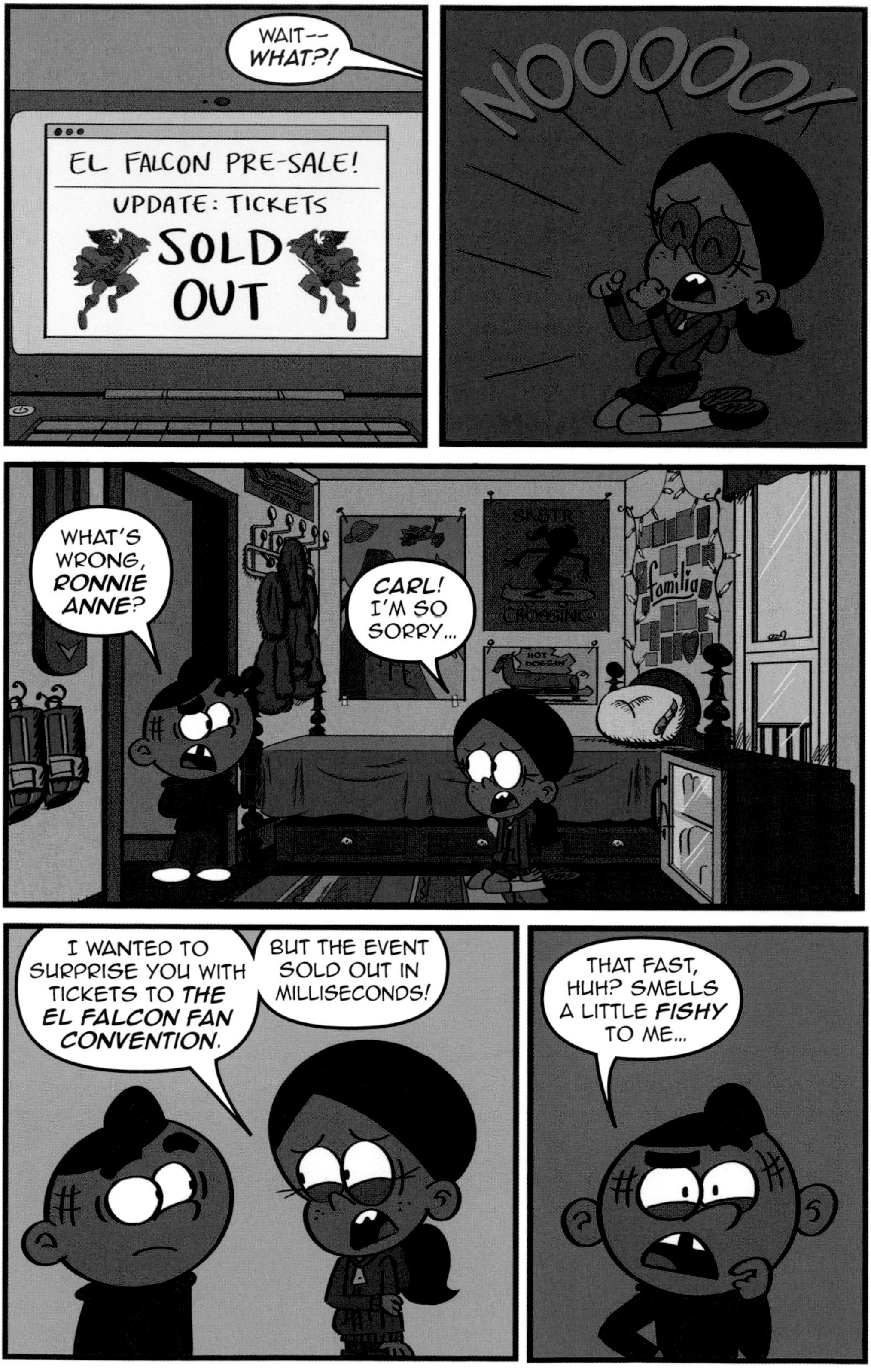
WAIT-- WHAT?!
EL FALCON PRE-SALE!
UPDATE: TICKETS
SOLD OUT
NOOOOO!
WHAT'S WRONG, RONNIE ANNE?
SK8TR
CROSSING
familia
HOT DOGGIN'
CARL! I'M SO SORRY...
I WANTED TO SURPRISE YOU WITH TICKETS TO THE EL FALCON FAN CONVENTION.
BUT THE EVENT SOLD OUT IN MILLISECONDS!
THAT FAST, HUH? SMELLS A LITTLE FISHY TO ME...

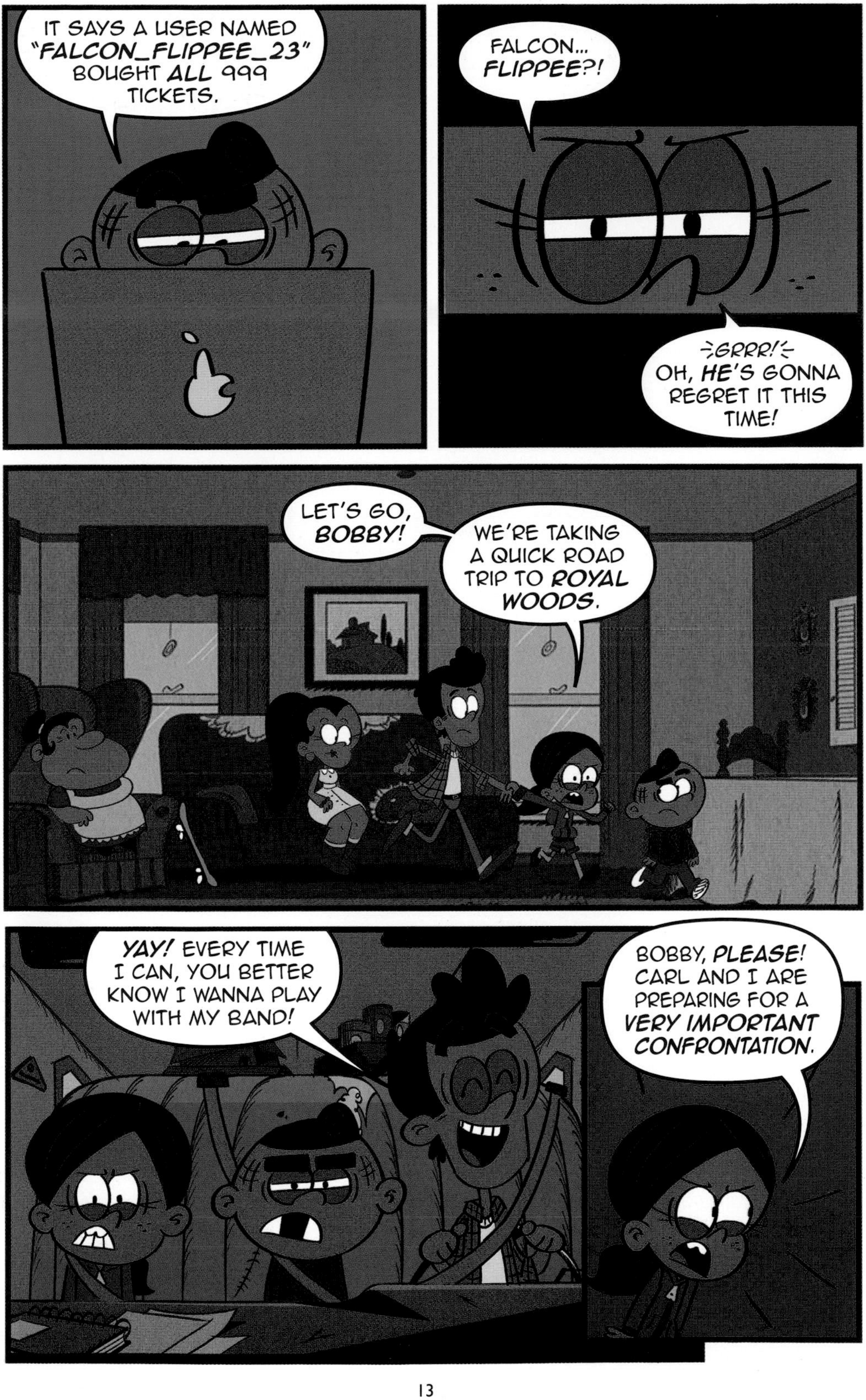
IT SAYS A USER NAMED "FALCON_FLIPPEE_23" BOUGHT ALL 999 TICKETS.
FALCON... FLIPPEE?!
GRRR! OH, HE'S GONNA REGRET IT THIS TIME!
LET'S GO, BOBBY!
WE'RE TAKING A QUICK ROAD TRIP TO ROYAL WOODS.
YAY! EVERY TIME I CAN, YOU BETTER KNOW I WANNA PLAY WITH MY BAND!
BOBBY, PLEASE! CARL AND I ARE PREPARING FOR A VERY IMPORTANT CONFRONTATION.

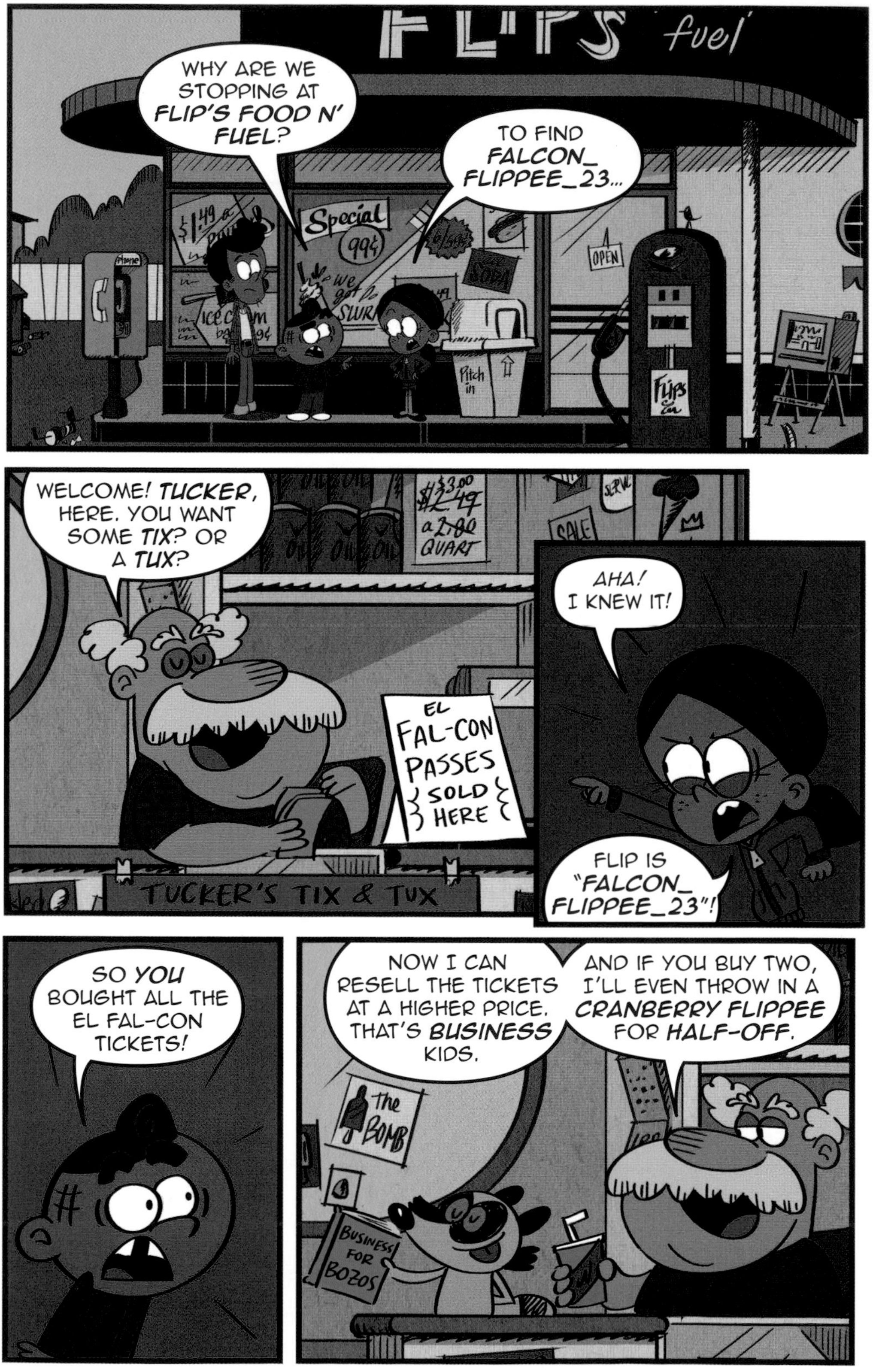

FLIP'S fuel
WHY ARE WE STOPPING AT FLIP'S FOOD N' FUEL?
TO FIND FALCON_ FLIPPEE_23...
Special 99¢
OPEN
Pitch in
WELCOME! TUCKER, HERE. YOU WANT SOME TIX? OR A TUX?
$3.00 a QUART
EL FAL-CON PASSES SOLD HERE
TUCKER'S TIX & TUX
AHA! I KNEW IT!
FLIP IS "FALCON_ FLIPPEE_23"!
SO YOU BOUGHT ALL THE EL FAL-CON TICKETS!
NOW I CAN RESELL THE TICKETS AT A HIGHER PRICE. THAT'S BUSINESS KIDS.
AND IF YOU BUY TWO, I'LL EVEN THROW IN A CRANBERRY FLIPPEE FOR HALF-OFF.
The BOMB
BUSINESS FOR BOZOS

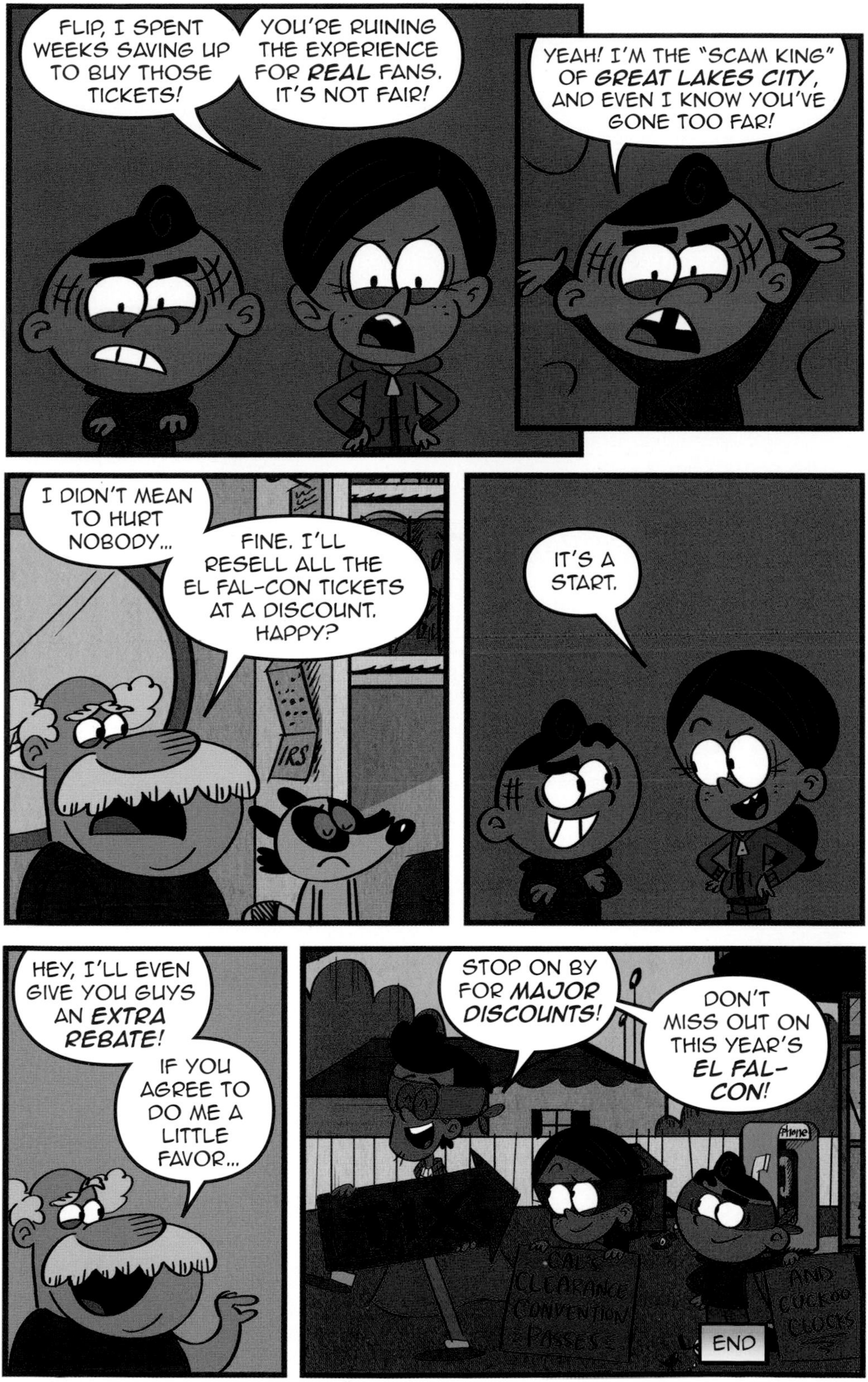
FLIP, I SPENT WEEKS SAVING UP TO BUY THOSE TICKETS!
YOU'RE RUINING THE EXPERIENCE FOR *REAL* FANS. IT'S NOT FAIR!
YEAH! I'M THE "SCAM KING" OF *GREAT LAKES CITY*, AND EVEN I KNOW YOU'VE GONE TOO FAR!
I DIDN'T MEAN TO HURT NOBODY...
FINE. I'LL RESELL ALL THE EL FAL-CON TICKETS AT A DISCOUNT. HAPPY?
IRS
IT'S A START.
HEY, I'LL EVEN GIVE YOU GUYS AN *EXTRA REBATE*!
IF YOU AGREE TO DO ME A LITTLE FAVOR...
STOP ON BY FOR *MAJOR DISCOUNTS*!
DON'T MISS OUT ON THIS YEAR'S *EL FAL-CON*!
Phone
CAL'S CLEARANCE CONVENTION PASSES
AND CUCKOO CLOCKS
END

"MARIACHI MIX-UP"

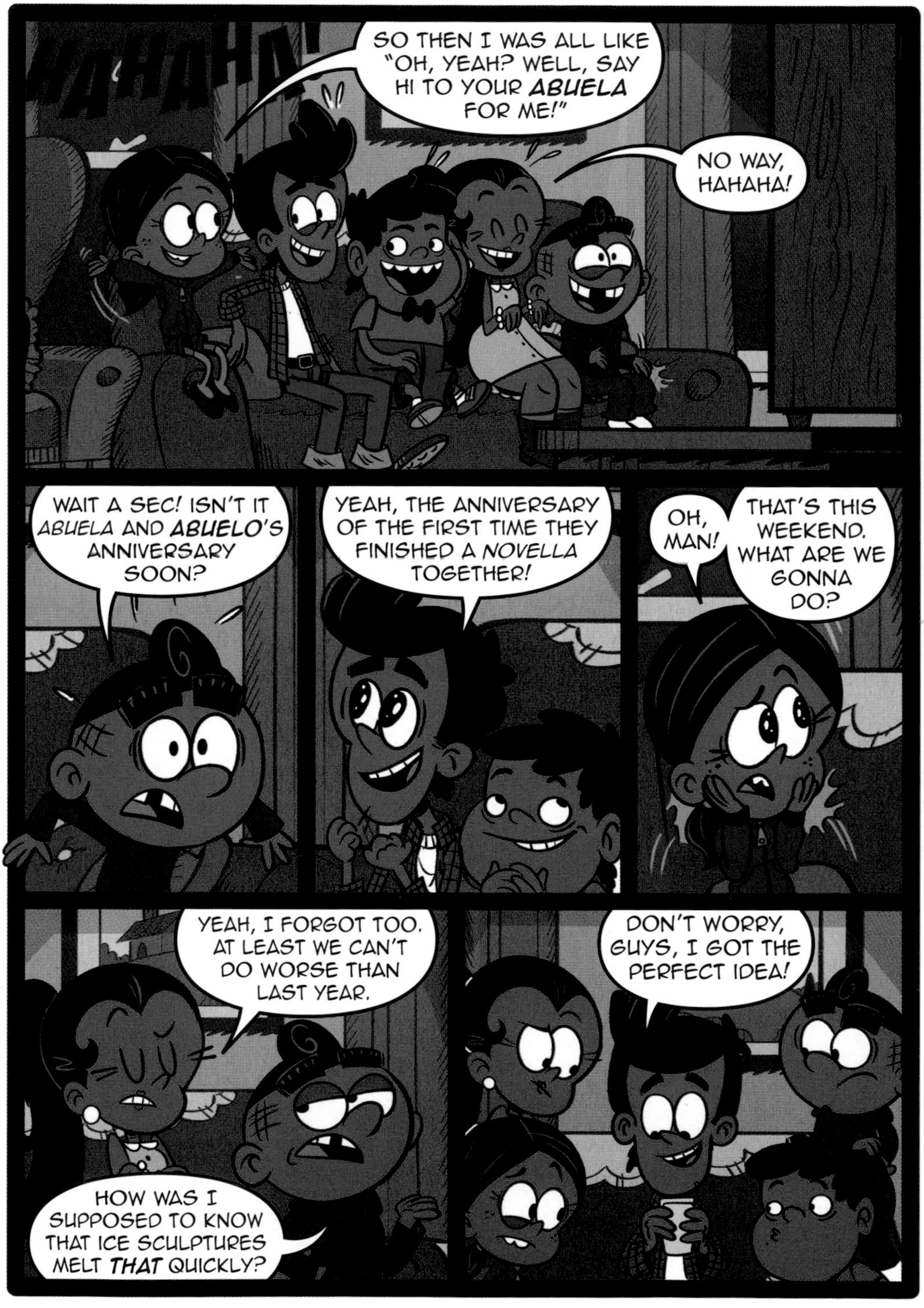
HAHAHA!
SO THEN I WAS ALL LIKE "OH, YEAH? WELL, SAY HI TO YOUR ABUELA FOR ME!"
NO WAY, HAHAHA!
WAIT A SEC! ISN'T IT ABUELA AND ABUELO'S ANNIVERSARY SOON?
YEAH, THE ANNIVERSARY OF THE FIRST TIME THEY FINISHED A NOVELLA TOGETHER!
OH, MAN!
THAT'S THIS WEEKEND. WHAT ARE WE GONNA DO?
YEAH, I FORGOT TOO. AT LEAST WE CAN'T DO WORSE THAN LAST YEAR.
HOW WAS I SUPPOSED TO KNOW THAT ICE SCULPTURES MELT THAT QUICKLY?
DON'T WORRY, GUYS, I GOT THE PERFECT IDEA!

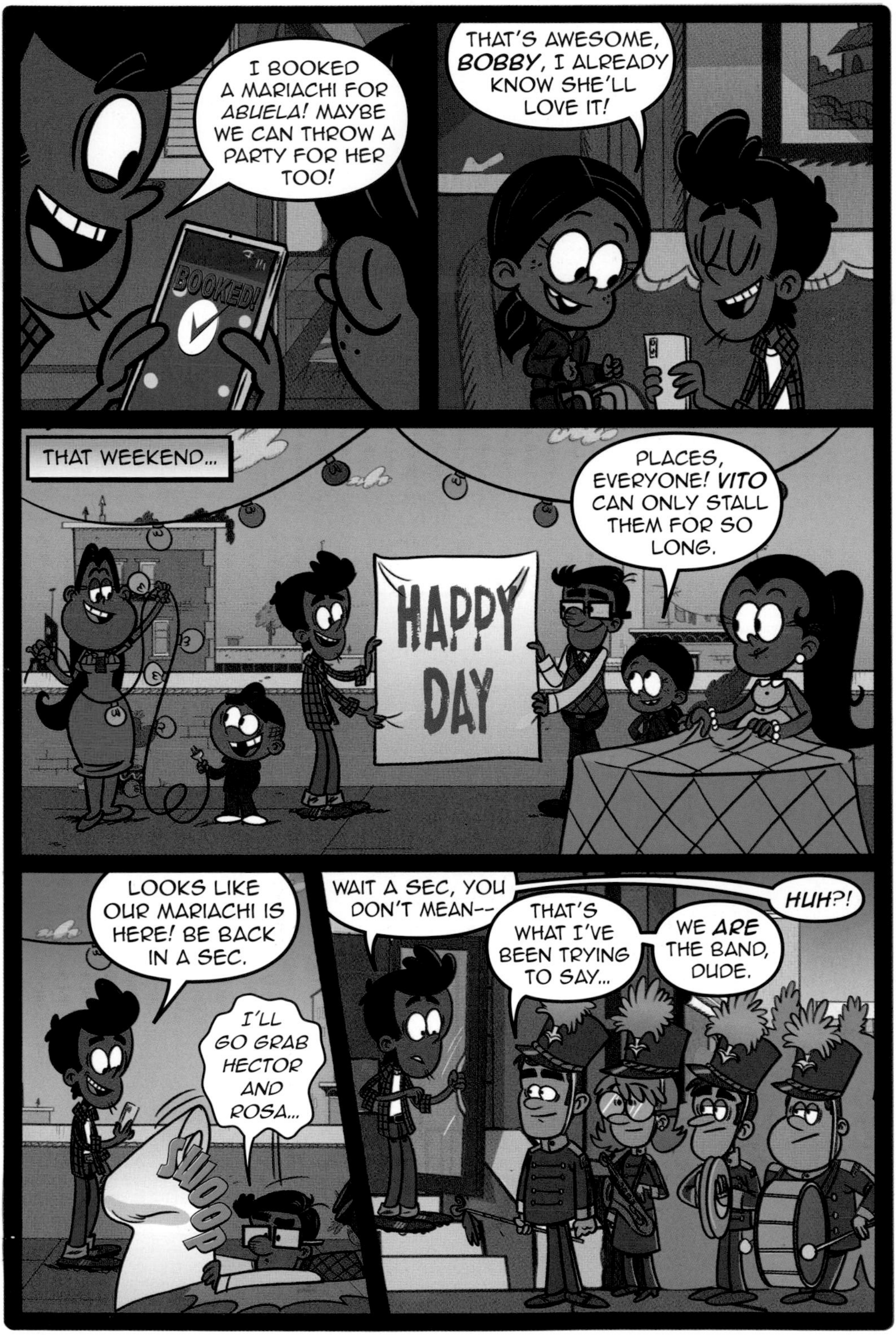
I BOOKED A MARIACHI FOR ABUELA! MAYBE WE CAN THROW A PARTY FOR HER TOO!
BOOKED!
THAT'S AWESOME, BOBBY, I ALREADY KNOW SHE'LL LOVE IT!
THAT WEEKEND...
PLACES, EVERYONE! VITO CAN ONLY STALL THEM FOR SO LONG.
HAPPY DAY
LOOKS LIKE OUR MARIACHI IS HERE! BE BACK IN A SEC.
I'LL GO GRAB HECTOR AND ROSA...
SWOOP
WAIT A SEC, YOU DON'T MEAN--
HUH?!
THAT'S WHAT I'VE BEEN TRYING TO SAY...
WE ARE THE BAND, DUDE.

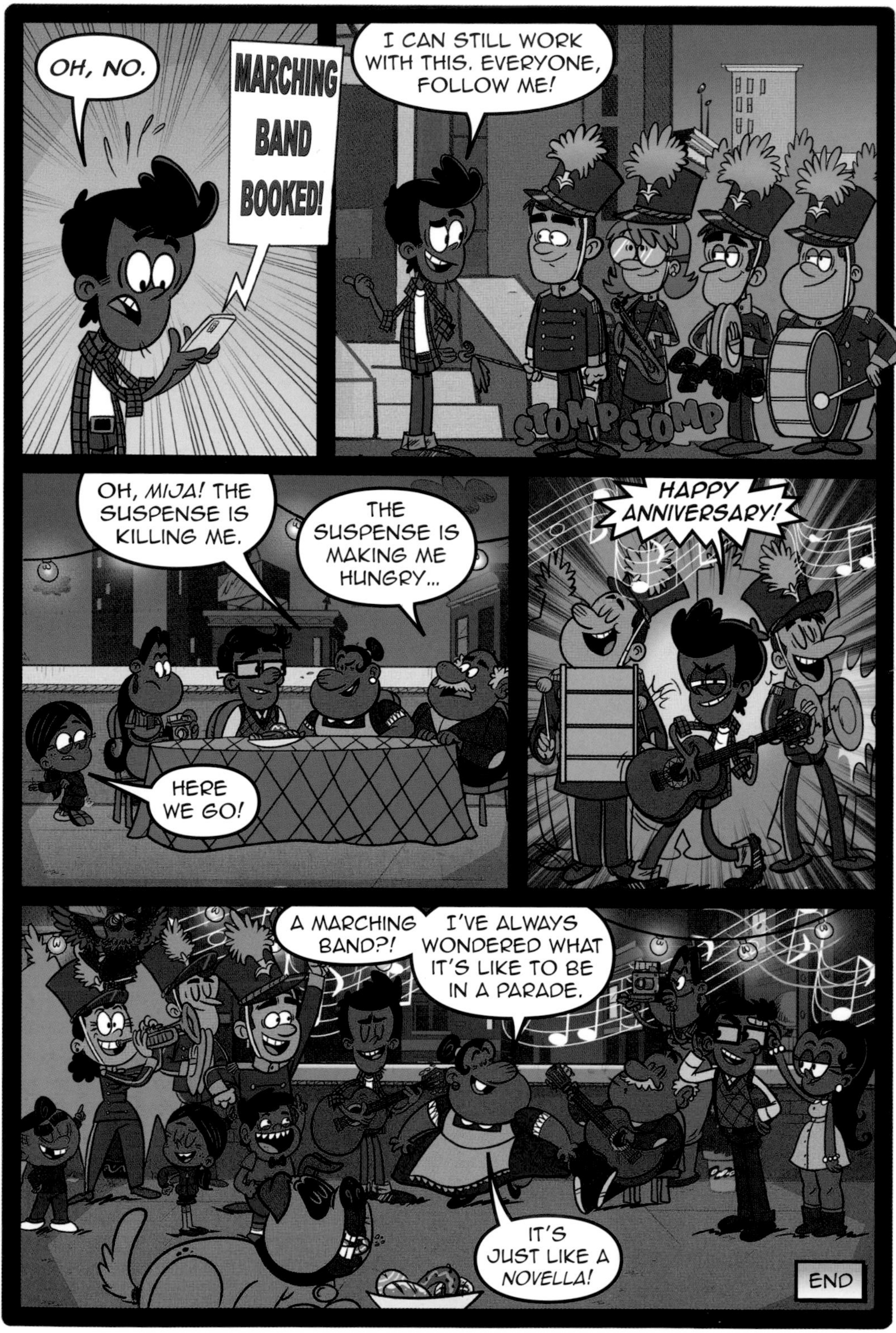

OH, NO.
MARCHING BAND BOOKED!
I CAN STILL WORK WITH THIS. EVERYONE, FOLLOW ME!
ZANG
STOMP STOMP
OH, *MIJA!* THE SUSPENSE IS KILLING ME.
THE SUSPENSE IS MAKING ME HUNGRY...
HERE WE GO!
HAPPY ANNIVERSARY!
A MARCHING BAND?!
I'VE ALWAYS WONDERED WHAT IT'S LIKE TO BE IN A PARADE.
IT'S JUST LIKE A *NOVELLA!*
END

"PUFF PIECE"

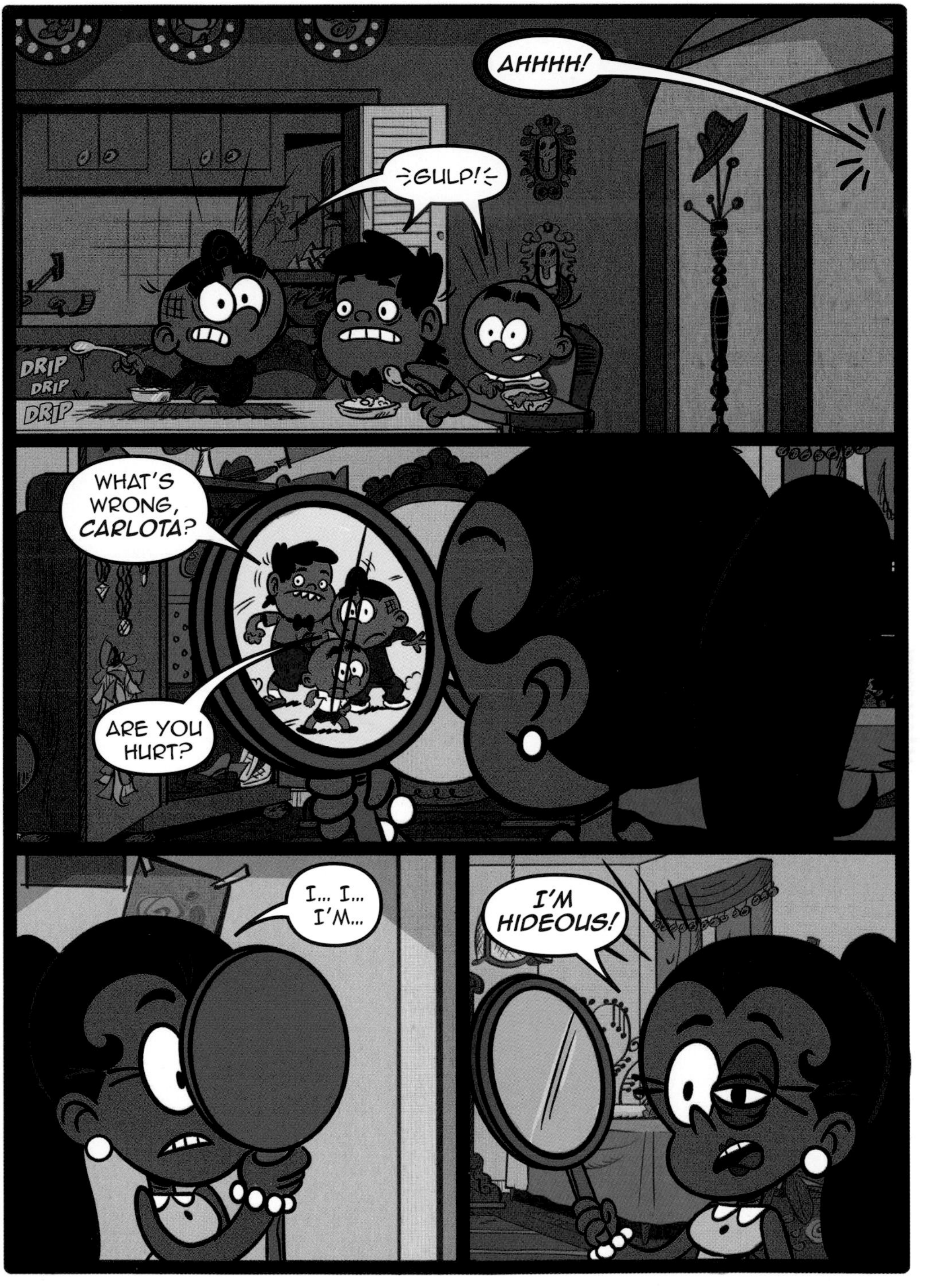
AHHHH!
GULP!
DRIP
DRIP
DRIP
WHAT'S WRONG, CARLOTA?
ARE YOU HURT?
I... I... I'M...
I'M HIDEOUS!

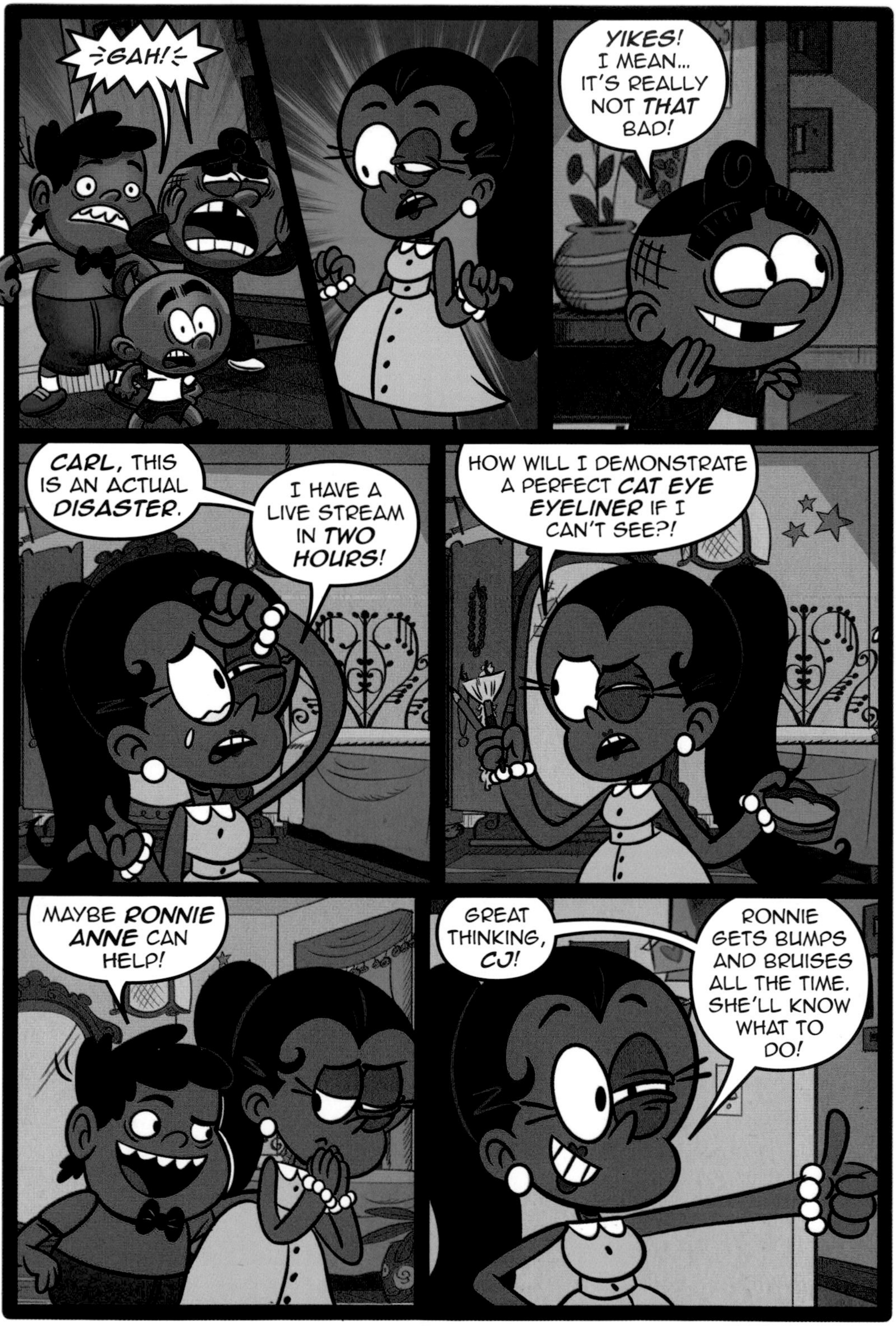
GAH!
YIKES! I MEAN... IT'S REALLY NOT THAT BAD!
CARL, THIS IS AN ACTUAL DISASTER.
I HAVE A LIVE STREAM IN TWO HOURS!
HOW WILL I DEMONSTRATE A PERFECT CAT EYE EYELINER IF I CAN'T SEE?!
MAYBE RONNIE ANNE CAN HELP!
GREAT THINKING, CJ!
RONNIE GETS BUMPS AND BRUISES ALL THE TIME. SHE'LL KNOW WHAT TO DO!

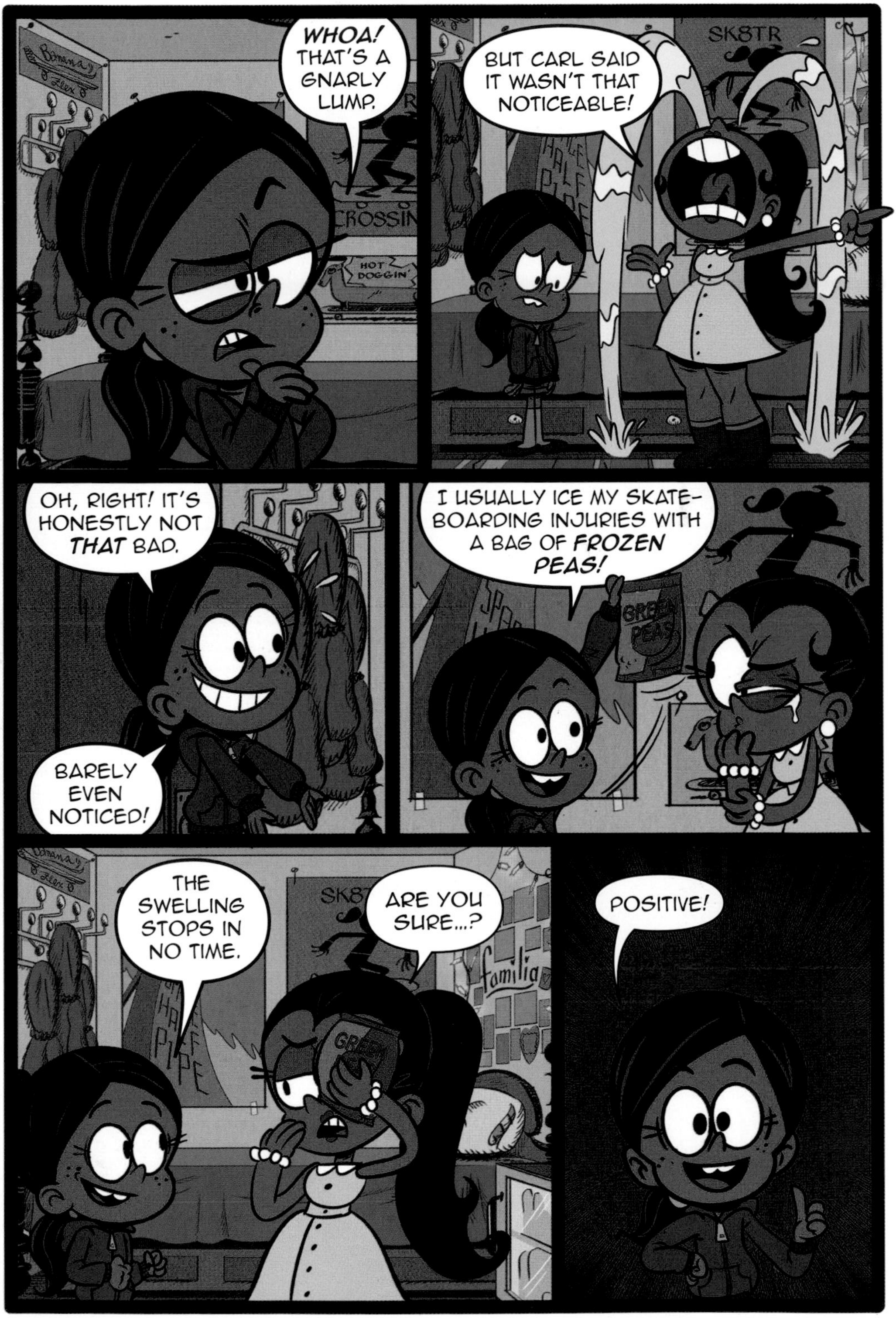
WHOA! THAT'S A GNARLY LUMP.
BUT CARL SAID IT WASN'T THAT NOTICEABLE!
OH, RIGHT! IT'S HONESTLY NOT THAT BAD.
BARELY EVEN NOTICED!
I USUALLY ICE MY SKATE-BOARDING INJURIES WITH A BAG OF FROZEN PEAS!
GREEN PEAS
THE SWELLING STOPS IN NO TIME.
ARE YOU SURE...?
POSITIVE!
SK8TR
CROSSIN
HOT DOGGIN'
HALF PIPE
familia

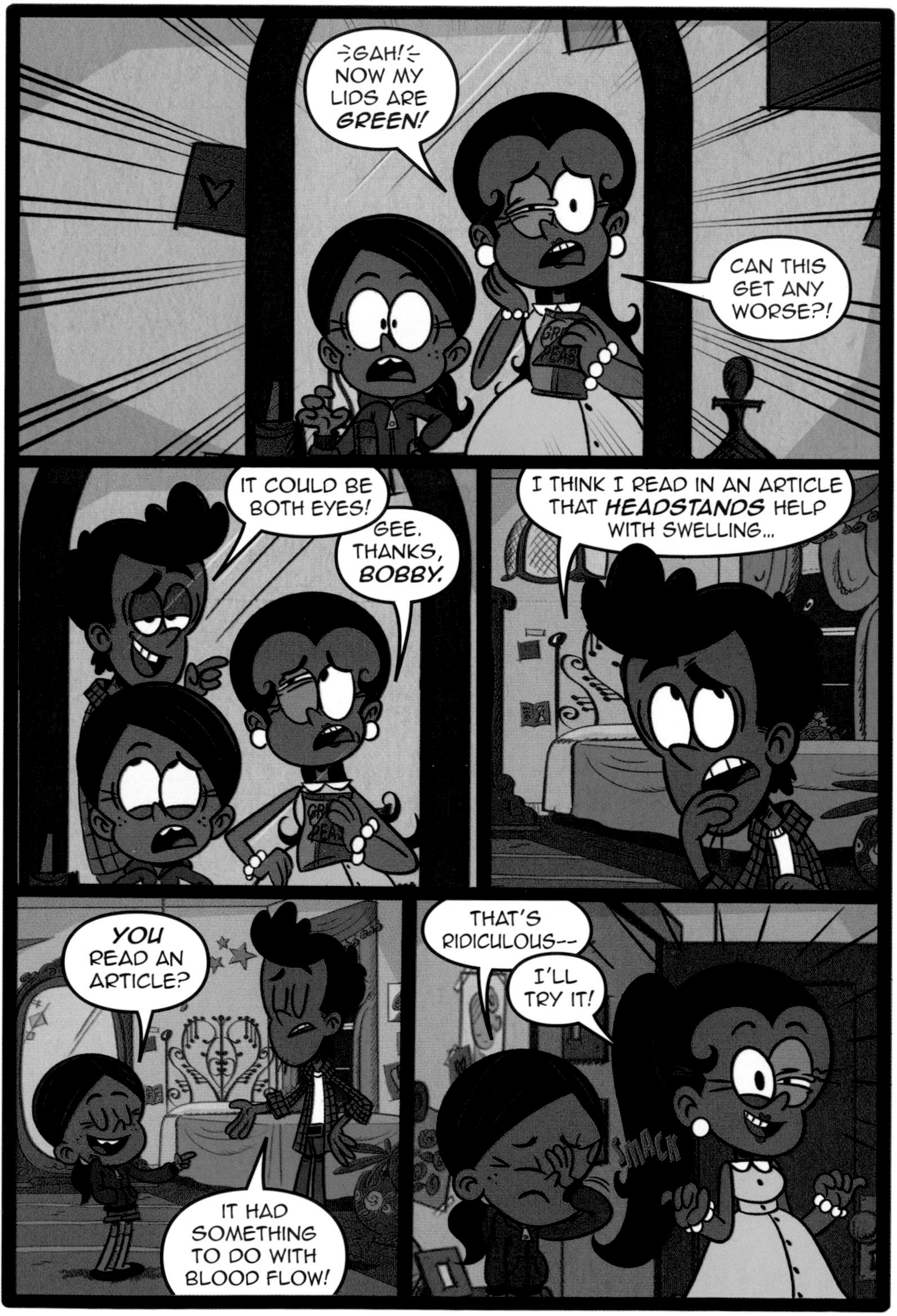
GAH! NOW MY LIDS ARE GREEN!
CAN THIS GET ANY WORSE?!
IT COULD BE BOTH EYES!
GEE. THANKS, BOBBY.
I THINK I READ IN AN ARTICLE THAT HEADSTANDS HELP WITH SWELLING...
YOU READ AN ARTICLE?
IT HAD SOMETHING TO DO WITH BLOOD FLOW!
THAT'S RIDICULOUS--
I'LL TRY IT!
SMACK

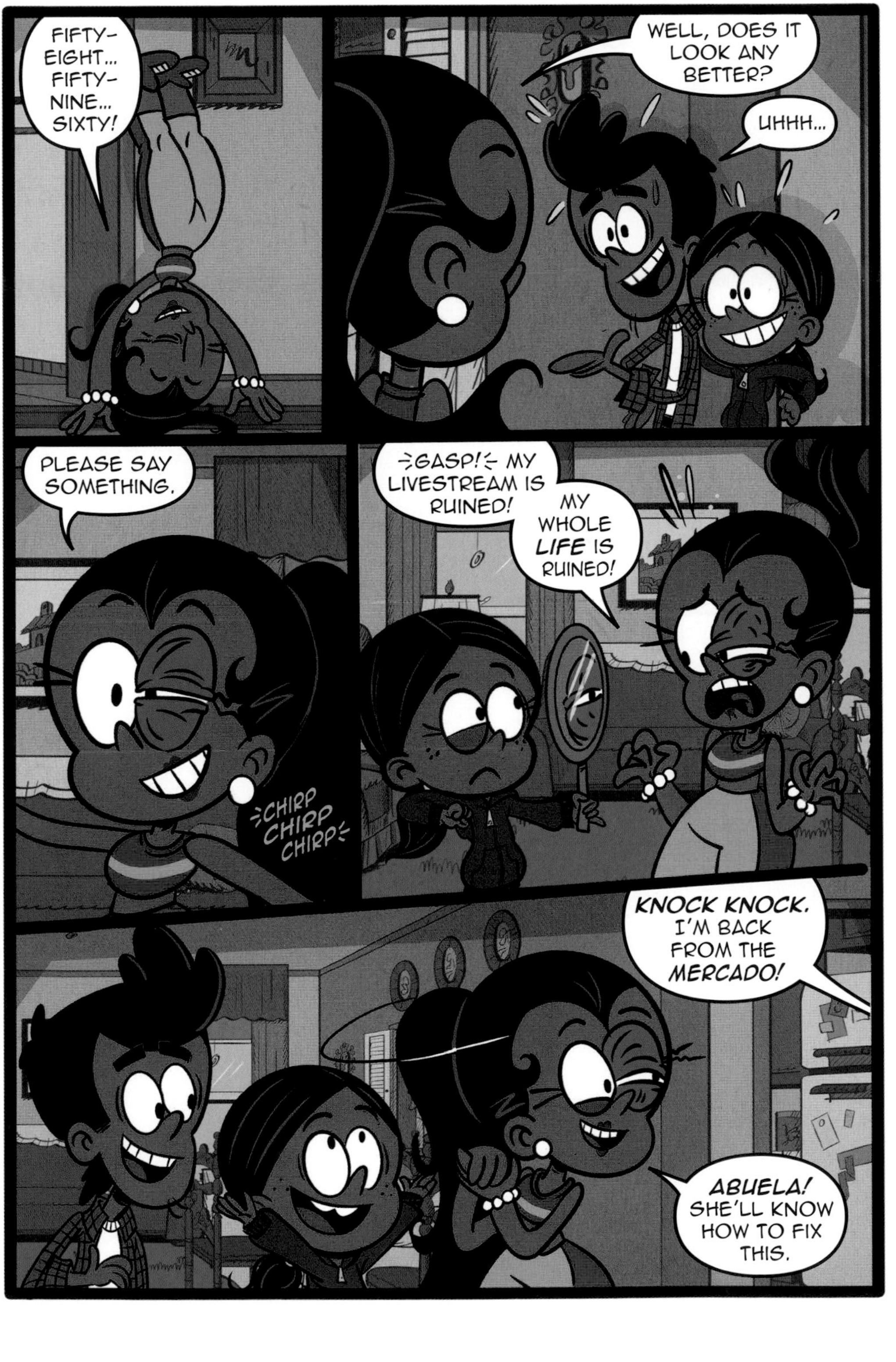
FIFTY-EIGHT... FIFTY-NINE... SIXTY!
WELL, DOES IT LOOK ANY BETTER?
UHHH...
PLEASE SAY SOMETHING.
CHIRP CHIRP CHIRP
GASP! MY LIVESTREAM IS RUINED!
MY WHOLE LIFE IS RUINED!
KNOCK KNOCK. I'M BACK FROM THE MERCADO!
ABUELA! SHE'LL KNOW HOW TO FIX THIS.

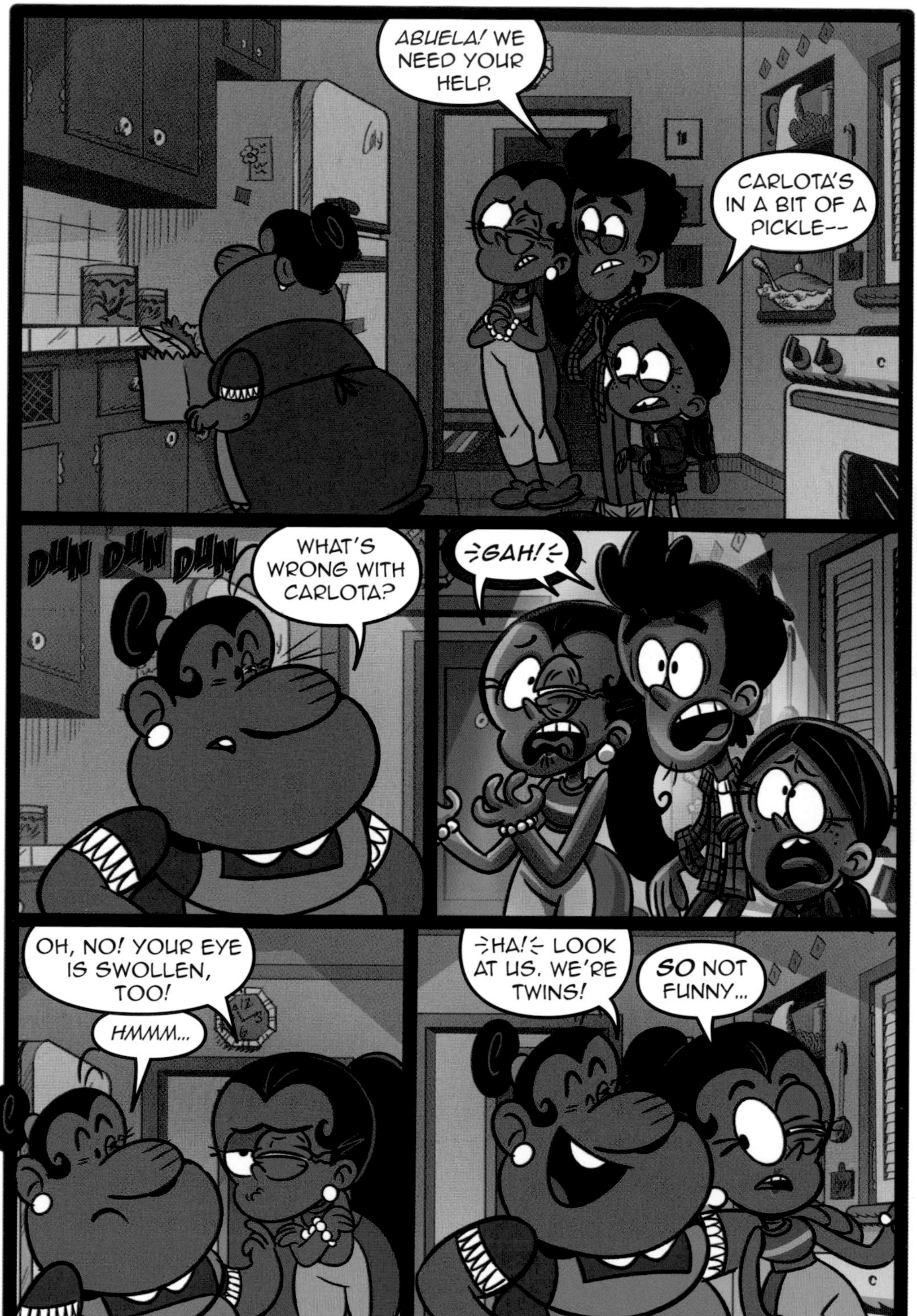
ABUELA! WE NEED YOUR HELP.
CARLOTA'S IN A BIT OF A PICKLE--
DUN DUN DUN
WHAT'S WRONG WITH CARLOTA?
GAH!
OH, NO! YOUR EYE IS SWOLLEN, TOO!
HMMM...
HA! LOOK AT US. WE'RE TWINS!
SO NOT FUNNY...

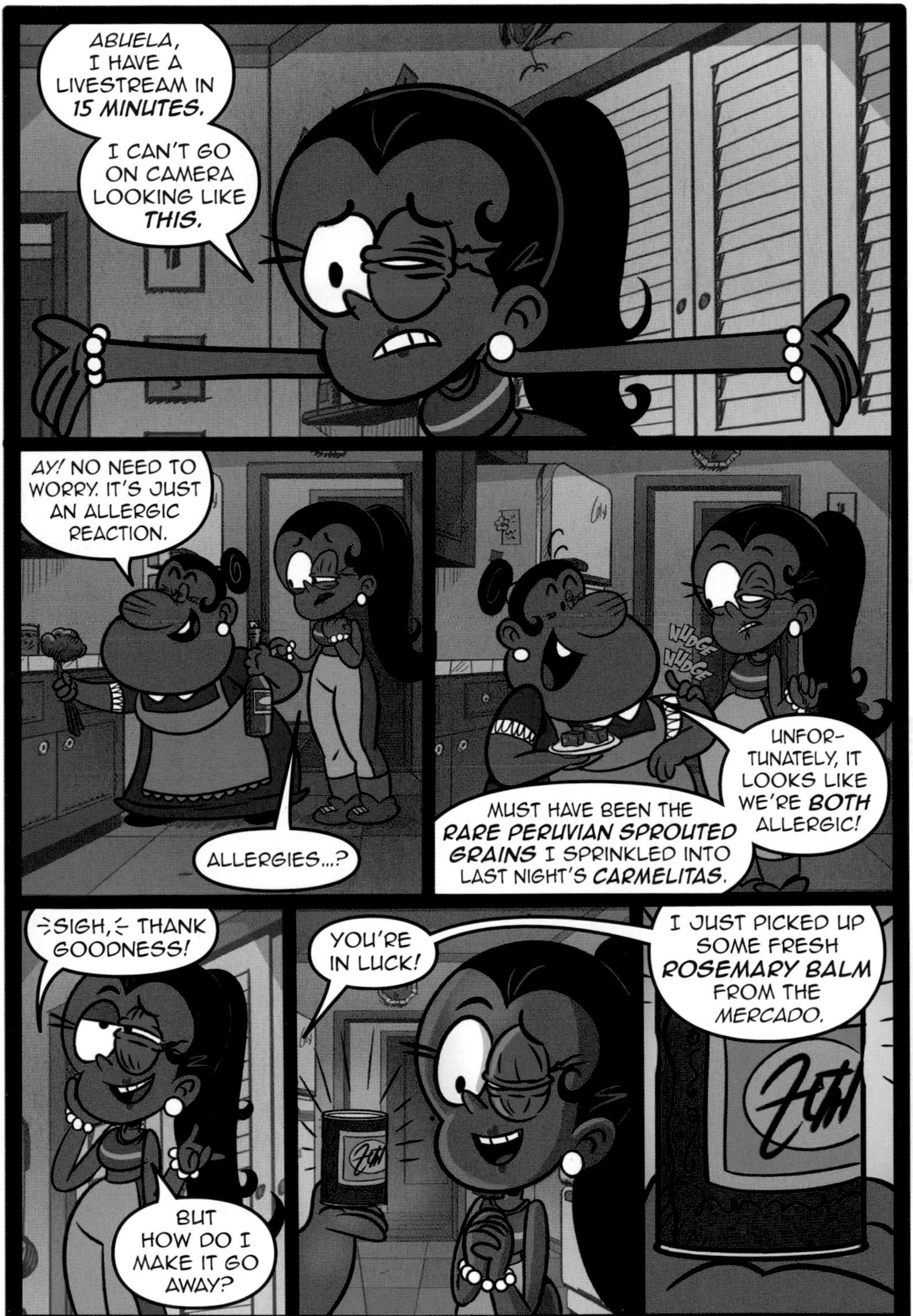
ABUELA, I HAVE A LIVESTREAM IN 15 MINUTES.
I CAN'T GO ON CAMERA LOOKING LIKE THIS.
AY! NO NEED TO WORRY. IT'S JUST AN ALLERGIC REACTION.
ALLERGIES...?
NUDGE NUDGE
MUST HAVE BEEN THE RARE PERUVIAN SPROUTED GRAINS I SPRINKLED INTO LAST NIGHT'S CARMELITAS.
UNFORTUNATELY, IT LOOKS LIKE WE'RE BOTH ALLERGIC!
SIGH, THANK GOODNESS!
BUT HOW DO I MAKE IT GO AWAY?
YOU'RE IN LUCK!
I JUST PICKED UP SOME FRESH ROSEMARY BALM FROM THE MERCADO.

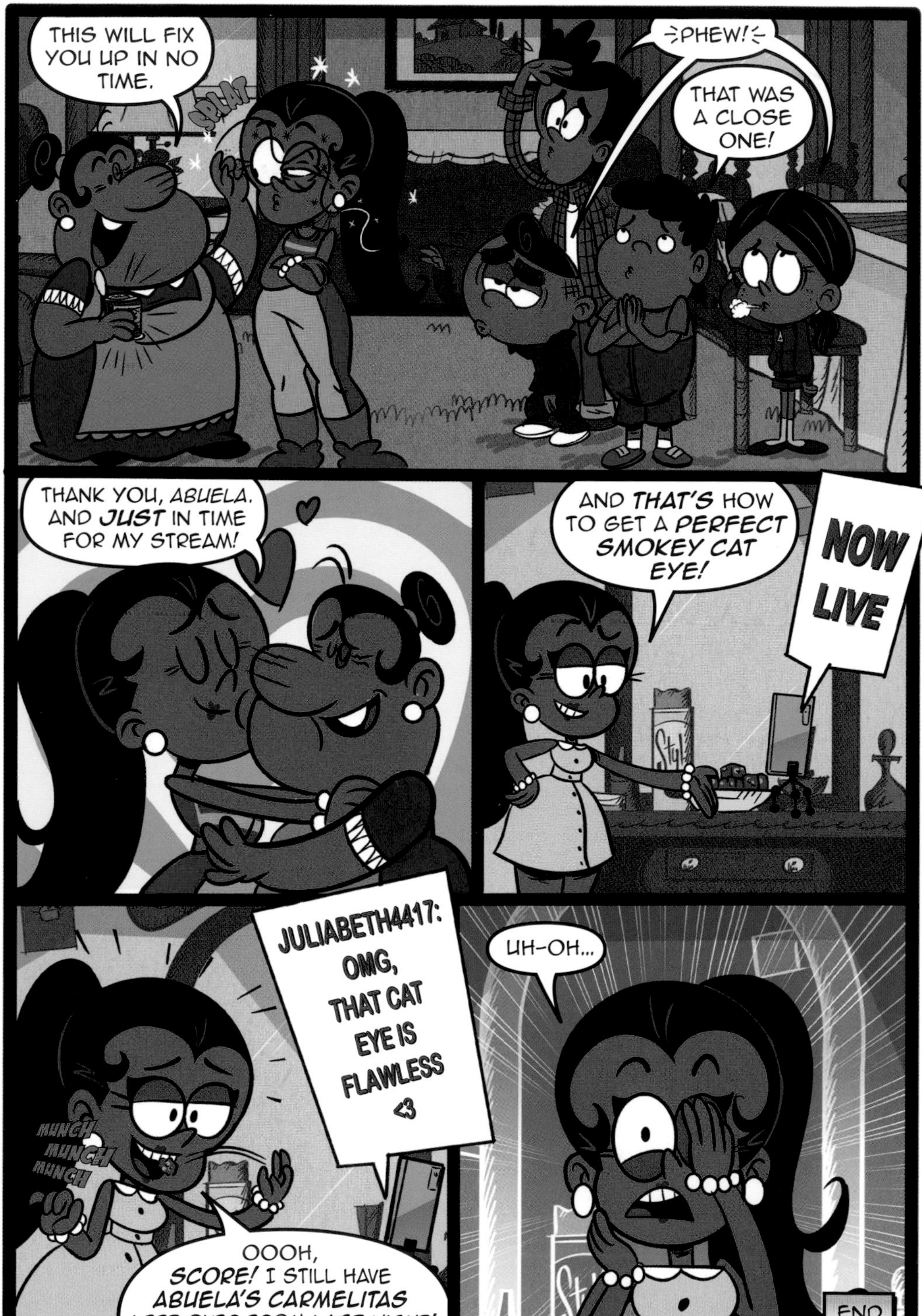
THIS WILL FIX YOU UP IN NO TIME.
SPLAT
PHEW!
THAT WAS A CLOSE ONE!
THANK YOU, ABUELA. AND JUST IN TIME FOR MY STREAM!
AND THAT'S HOW TO GET A PERFECT SMOKEY CAT EYE!
NOW LIVE
JULIABETH4417: OMG, THAT CAT EYE IS FLAWLESS <3
MUNCH MUNCH MUNCH
OOOH, SCORE! I STILL HAVE ABUELA'S CARMELITAS LEFT OVER FROM LAST NIGHT!
UH-OH...
END

"THE DOCTOR IS IN"

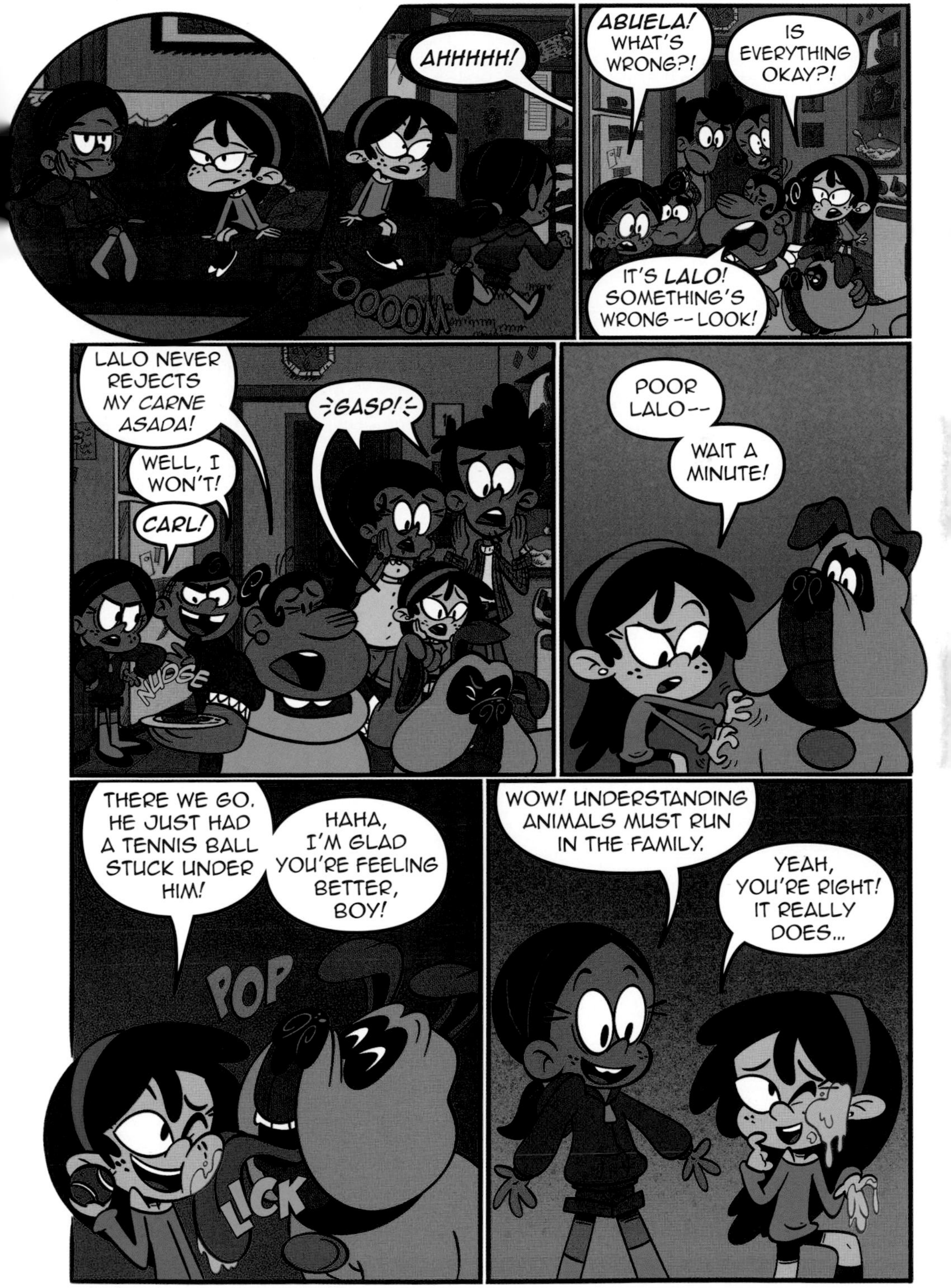
AHHHHH!
ZOOOOM
ABUELA! WHAT'S WRONG?!
IS EVERYTHING OKAY?!
IT'S LALO! SOMETHING'S WRONG -- LOOK!
LALO NEVER REJECTS MY CARNE ASADA!
GASP!
WELL, I WON'T!
CARL!
NUDGE
POOR LALO--
WAIT A MINUTE!
THERE WE GO. HE JUST HAD A TENNIS BALL STUCK UNDER HIM!
HAHA, I'M GLAD YOU'RE FEELING BETTER, BOY!
POP
LICK
WOW! UNDERSTANDING ANIMALS MUST RUN IN THE FAMILY.
YEAH, YOU'RE RIGHT! IT REALLY DOES...

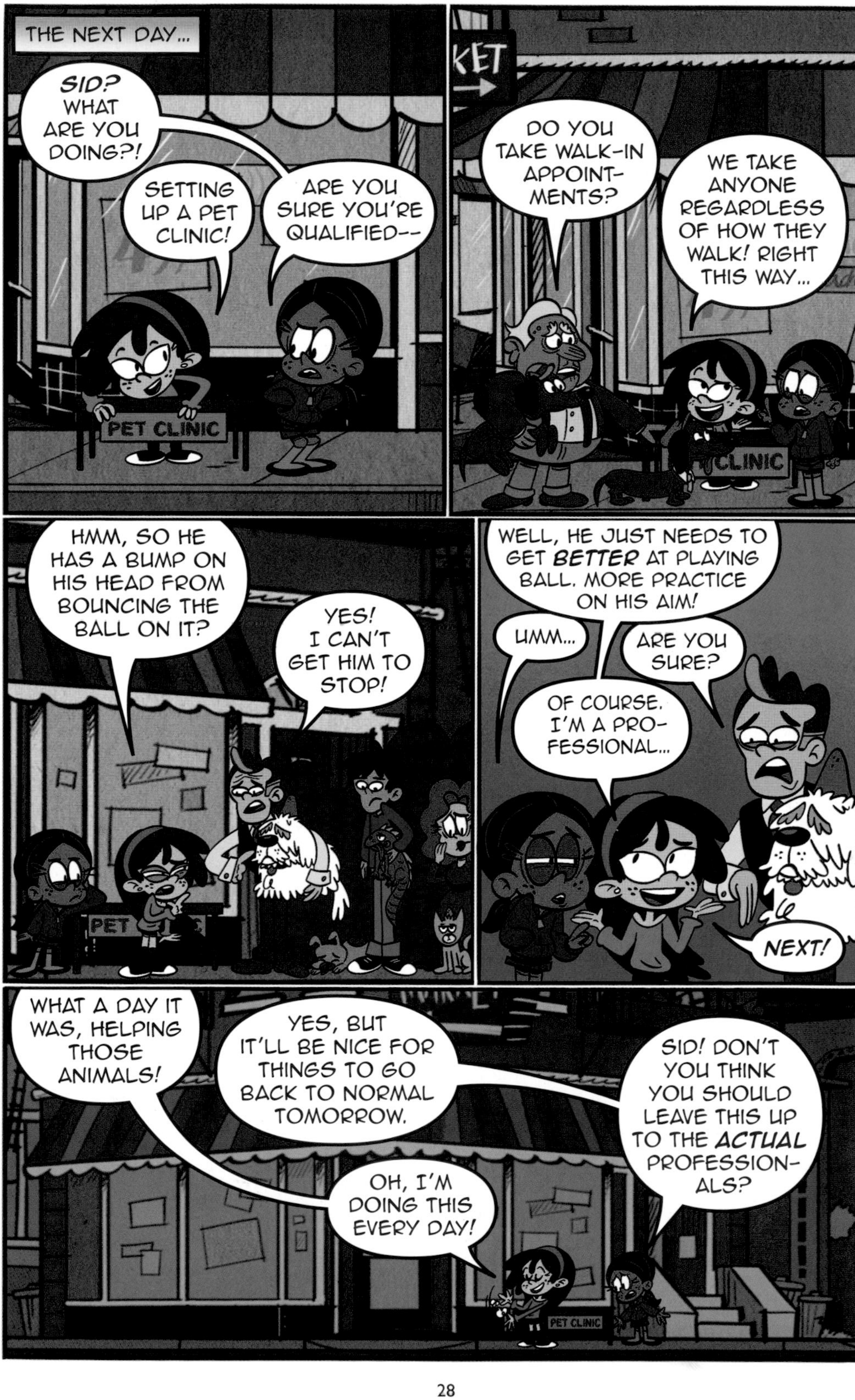
THE NEXT DAY...
SID? WHAT ARE YOU DOING?!
SETTING UP A PET CLINIC!
ARE YOU SURE YOU'RE QUALIFIED--
PET CLINIC
DO YOU TAKE WALK-IN APPOINT-MENTS?
WE TAKE ANYONE REGARDLESS OF HOW THEY WALK! RIGHT THIS WAY...
HMM, SO HE HAS A BUMP ON HIS HEAD FROM BOUNCING THE BALL ON IT?
YES! I CAN'T GET HIM TO STOP!
WELL, HE JUST NEEDS TO GET BETTER AT PLAYING BALL. MORE PRACTICE ON HIS AIM!
UMM...
ARE YOU SURE?
OF COURSE. I'M A PRO-FESSIONAL...
NEXT!
WHAT A DAY IT WAS, HELPING THOSE ANIMALS!
YES, BUT IT'LL BE NICE FOR THINGS TO GO BACK TO NORMAL TOMORROW.
OH, I'M DOING THIS EVERY DAY!
SID! DON'T YOU THINK YOU SHOULD LEAVE THIS UP TO THE ACTUAL PROFESSION-ALS?
PET CLINIC

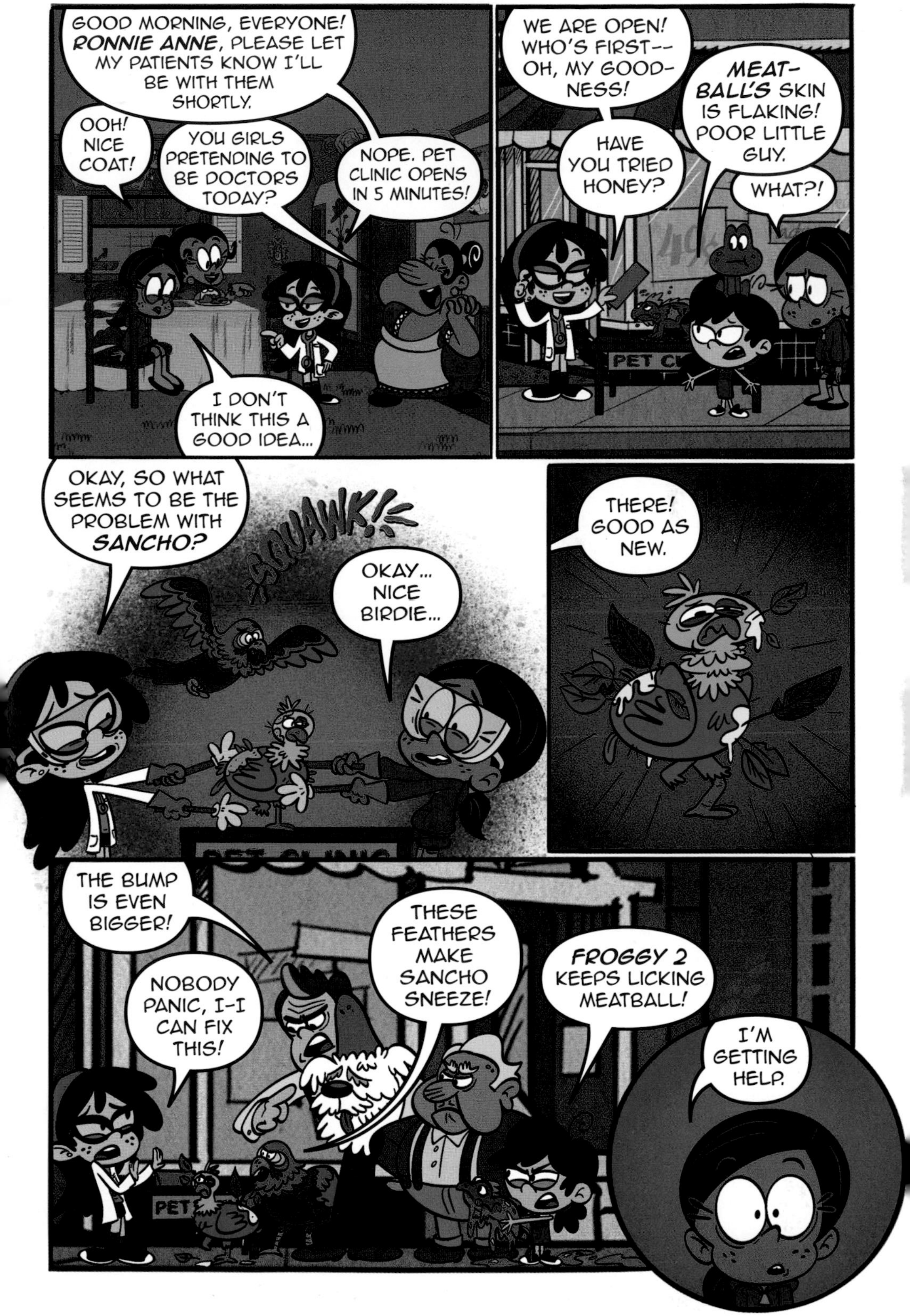
GOOD MORNING, EVERYONE! RONNIE ANNE, PLEASE LET MY PATIENTS KNOW I'LL BE WITH THEM SHORTLY.
OOH! NICE COAT!
YOU GIRLS PRETENDING TO BE DOCTORS TODAY?
NOPE. PET CLINIC OPENS IN 5 MINUTES!
I DON'T THINK THIS A GOOD IDEA...
WE ARE OPEN! WHO'S FIRST-- OH, MY GOOD-NESS!
MEAT-BALL'S SKIN IS FLAKING! POOR LITTLE GUY.
HAVE YOU TRIED HONEY?
WHAT?!
PET C
OKAY, SO WHAT SEEMS TO BE THE PROBLEM WITH SANCHO?
SQUAWK!
OKAY... NICE BIRDIE...
THERE! GOOD AS NEW.
THE BUMP IS EVEN BIGGER!
NOBODY PANIC, I-I CAN FIX THIS!
THESE FEATHERS MAKE SANCHO SNEEZE!
FROGGY 2 KEEPS LICKING MEATBALL!
I'M GETTING HELP.
PET

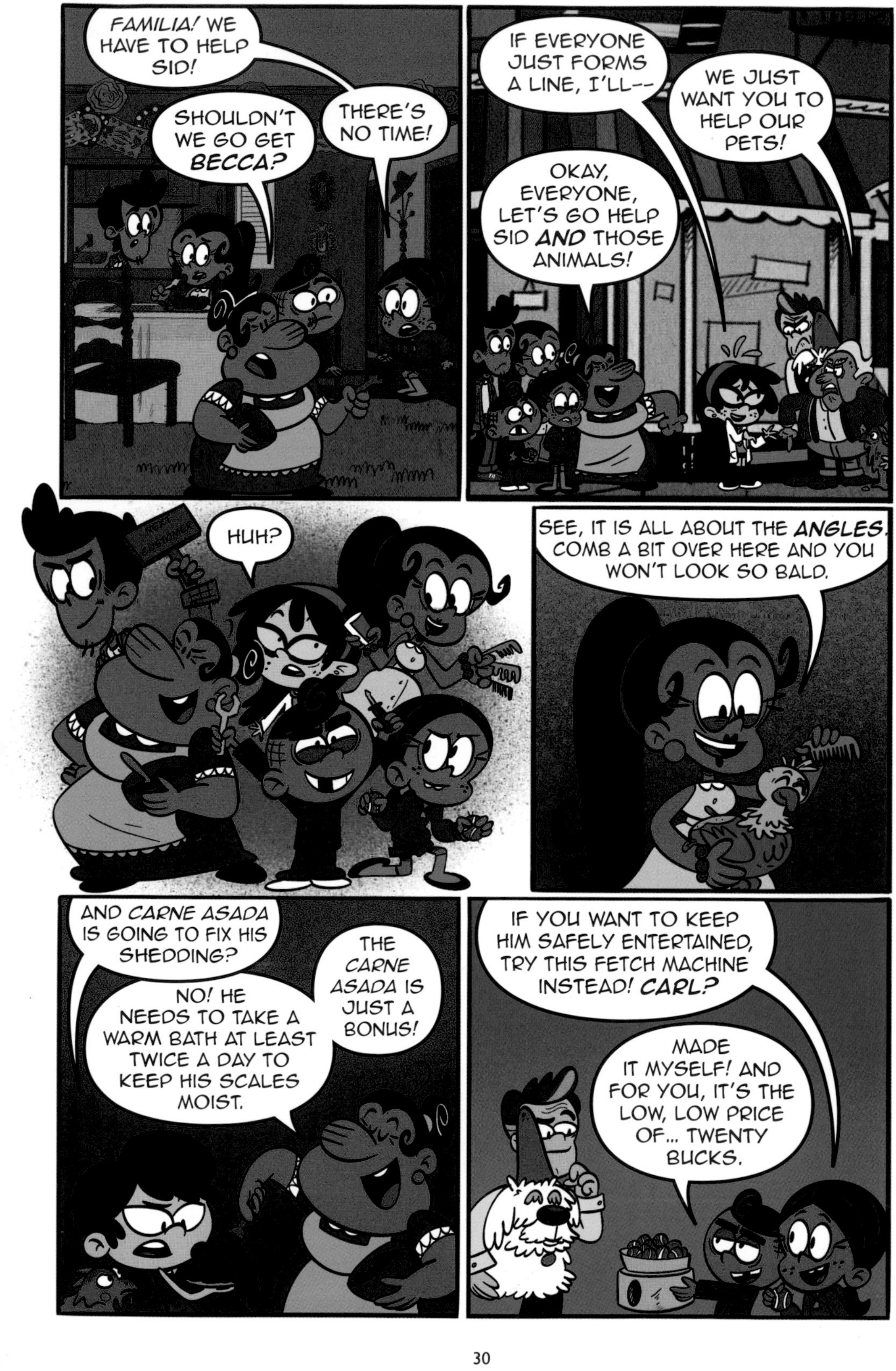
FAMILIA! WE HAVE TO HELP SID!
SHOULDN'T WE GO GET BECCA?
THERE'S NO TIME!
IF EVERYONE JUST FORMS A LINE, I'LL--
WE JUST WANT YOU TO HELP OUR PETS!
OKAY, EVERYONE, LET'S GO HELP SID AND THOSE ANIMALS!
HUH?
SEE, IT IS ALL ABOUT THE ANGLES! COMB A BIT OVER HERE AND YOU WON'T LOOK SO BALD.
AND CARNE ASADA IS GOING TO FIX HIS SHEDDING?
NO! HE NEEDS TO TAKE A WARM BATH AT LEAST TWICE A DAY TO KEEP HIS SCALES MOIST.
THE CARNE ASADA IS JUST A BONUS!
IF YOU WANT TO KEEP HIM SAFELY ENTERTAINED, TRY THIS FETCH MACHINE INSTEAD! CARL?
MADE IT MYSELF! AND FOR YOU, IT'S THE LOW, LOW PRICE OF... TWENTY BUCKS.

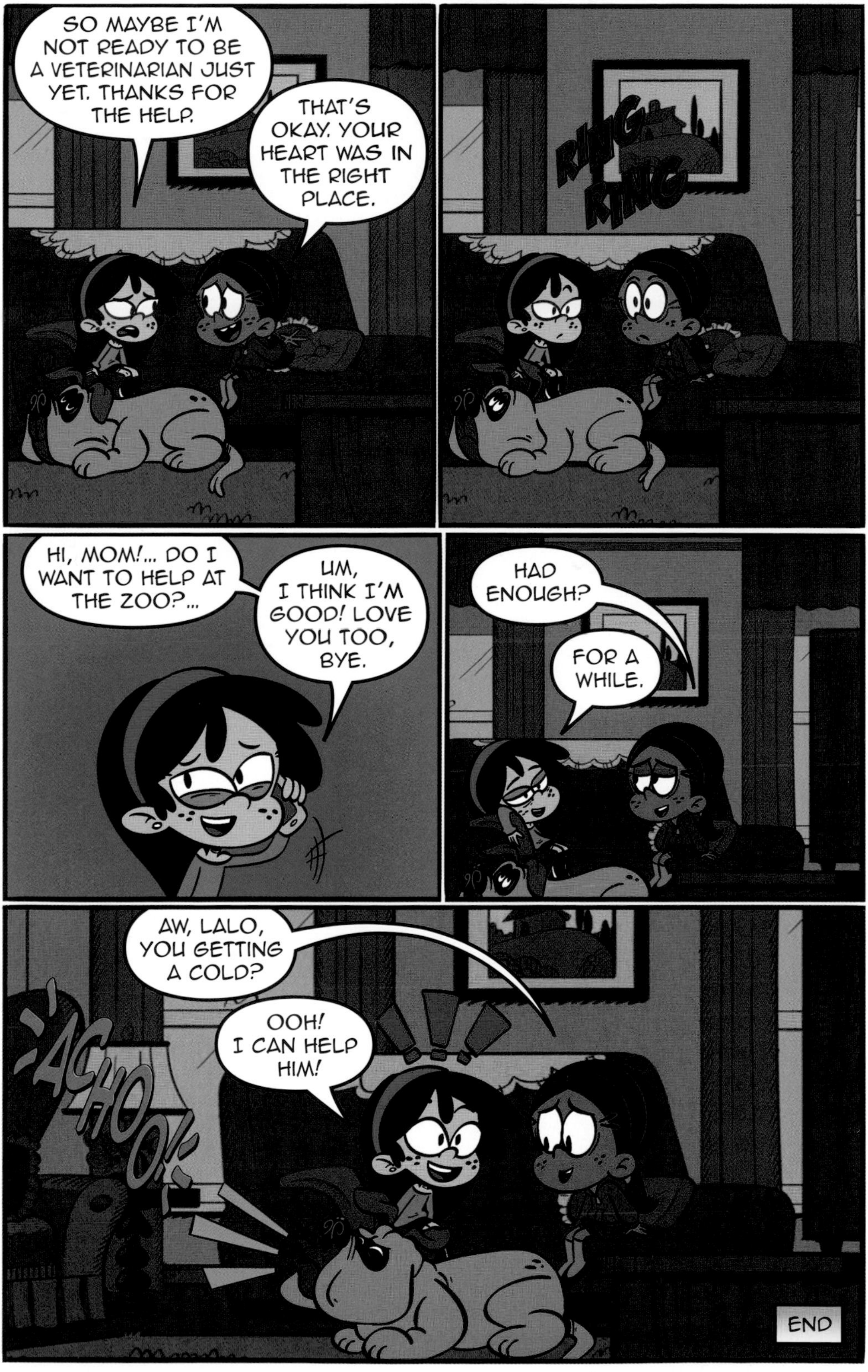
SO MAYBE I'M NOT READY TO BE A VETERINARIAN JUST YET. THANKS FOR THE HELP.
THAT'S OKAY. YOUR HEART WAS IN THE RIGHT PLACE.
RING RING
HI, MOM!... DO I WANT TO HELP AT THE ZOO?...
UM, I THINK I'M GOOD! LOVE YOU TOO, BYE.
HAD ENOUGH?
FOR A WHILE.
AW, LALO, YOU GETTING A COLD?
ACHOO!
OOH! I CAN HELP HIM!
END

"BABY MAKES BANK"

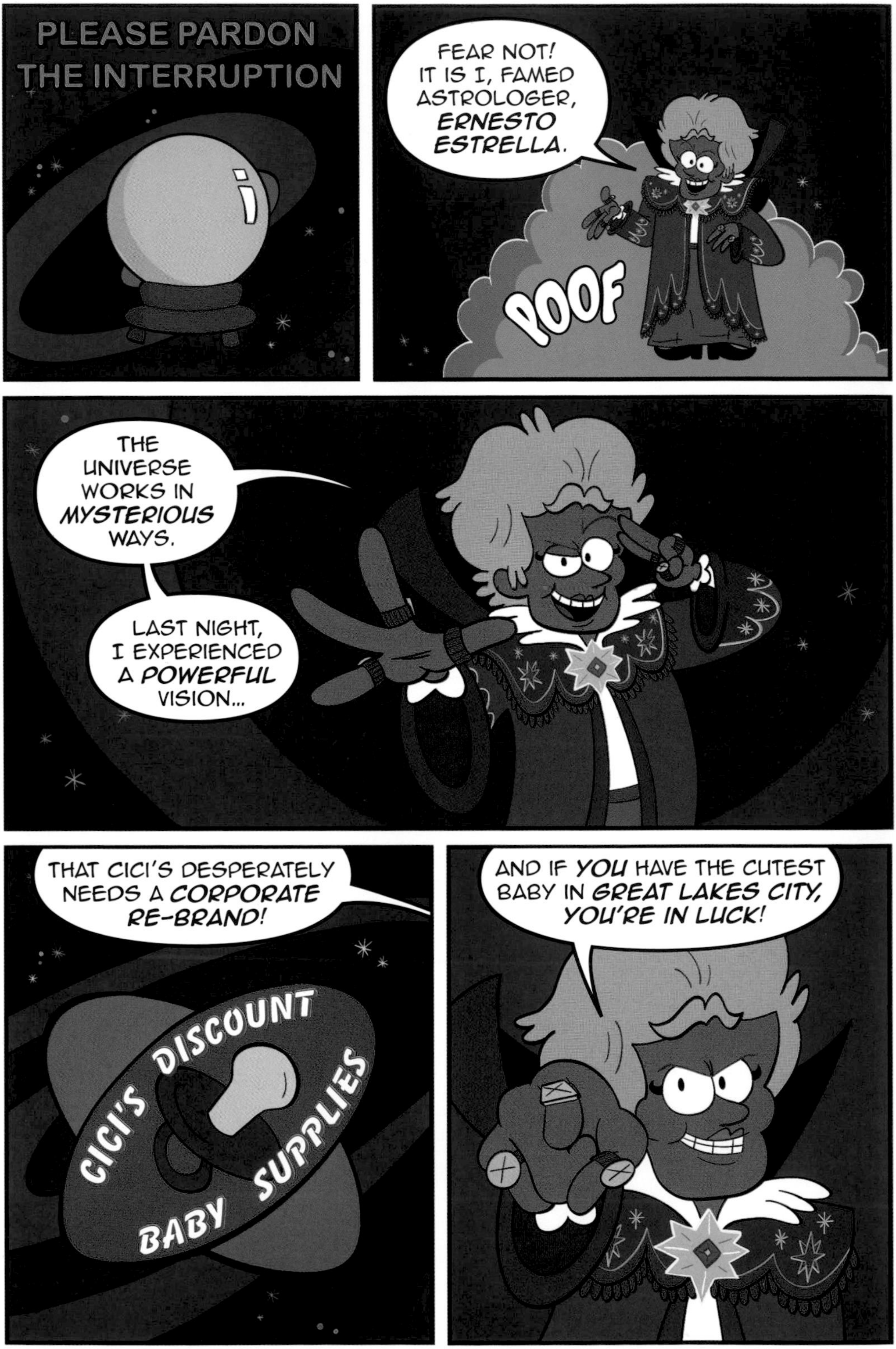
PLEASE PARDON THE INTERRUPTION
FEAR NOT! IT IS I, FAMED ASTROLOGER, ERNESTO ESTRELLA.
POOF
THE UNIVERSE WORKS IN MYSTERIOUS WAYS.
LAST NIGHT, I EXPERIENCED A POWERFUL VISION...
THAT CICI'S DESPERATELY NEEDS A CORPORATE RE-BRAND!
CICI'S DISCOUNT BABY SUPPLIES
AND IF YOU HAVE THE CUTEST BABY IN GREAT LAKES CITY, YOU'RE IN LUCK!

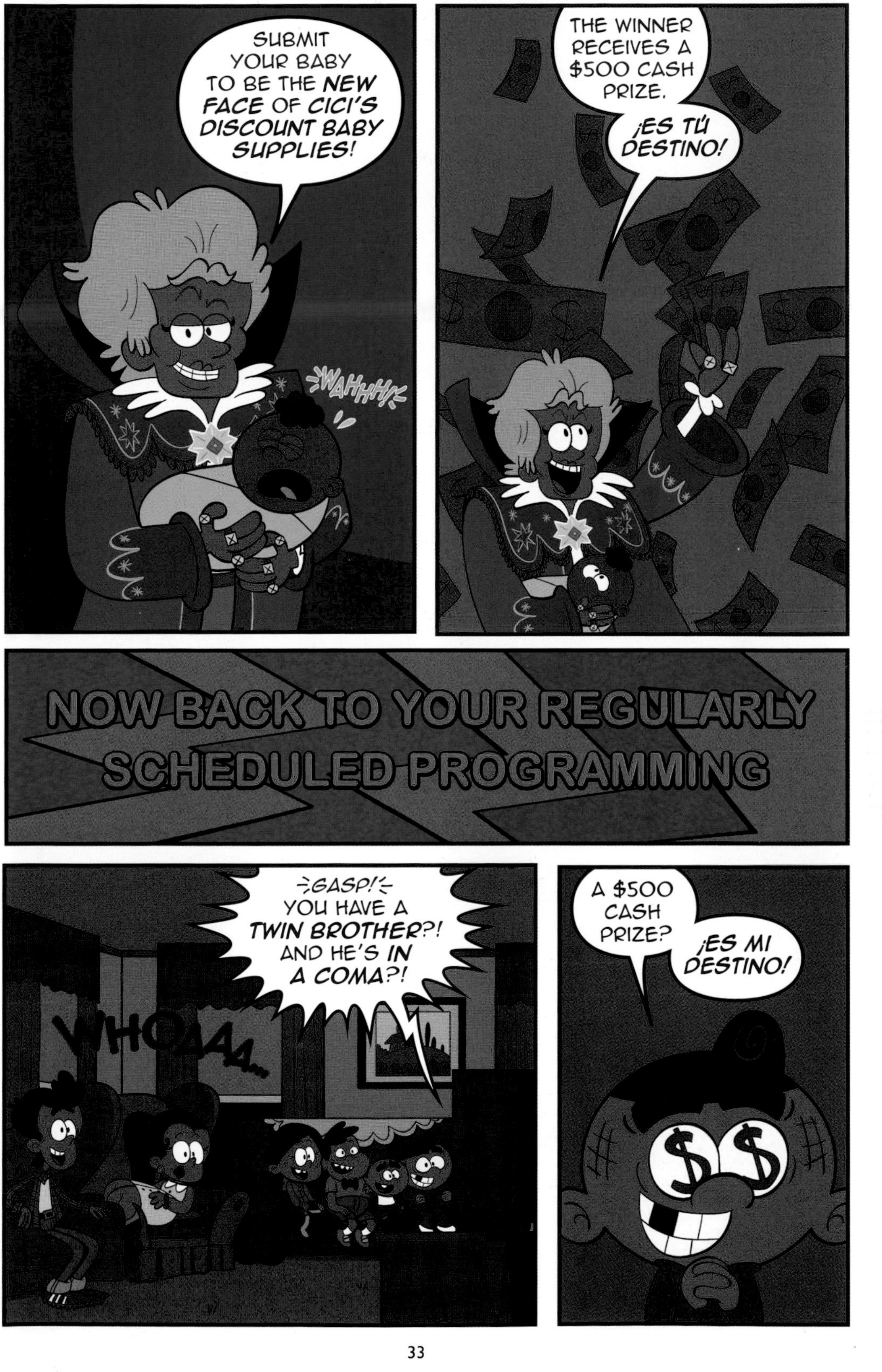

SUBMIT YOUR BABY TO BE THE NEW FACE OF CICI'S DISCOUNT BABY SUPPLIES!
WAHHH!
THE WINNER RECEIVES A $500 CASH PRIZE.
¡ES TÚ DESTINO!
NOW BACK TO YOUR REGULARLY SCHEDULED PROGRAMMING
GASP! YOU HAVE A TWIN BROTHER?! AND HE'S IN A COMA?!
WHOAAA...
A $500 CASH PRIZE?
¡ES MI DESTINO!

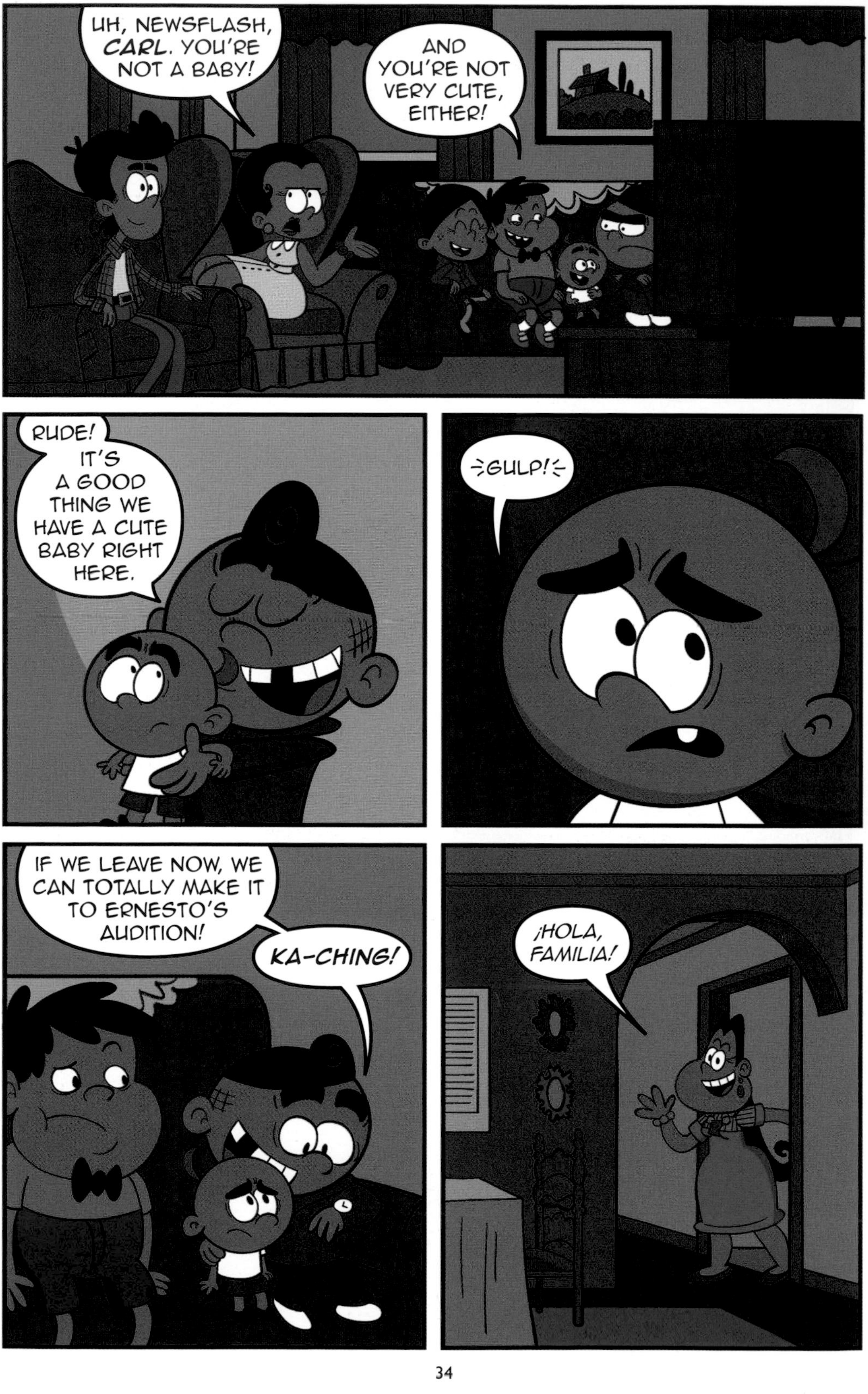
UH, NEWSFLASH, CARL. YOU'RE NOT A BABY!
AND YOU'RE NOT VERY CUTE, EITHER!
RUDE!
IT'S A GOOD THING WE HAVE A CUTE BABY RIGHT HERE.
GULP!
IF WE LEAVE NOW, WE CAN TOTALLY MAKE IT TO ERNESTO'S AUDITION!
KA-CHING!
¡HOLA, FAMILIA!

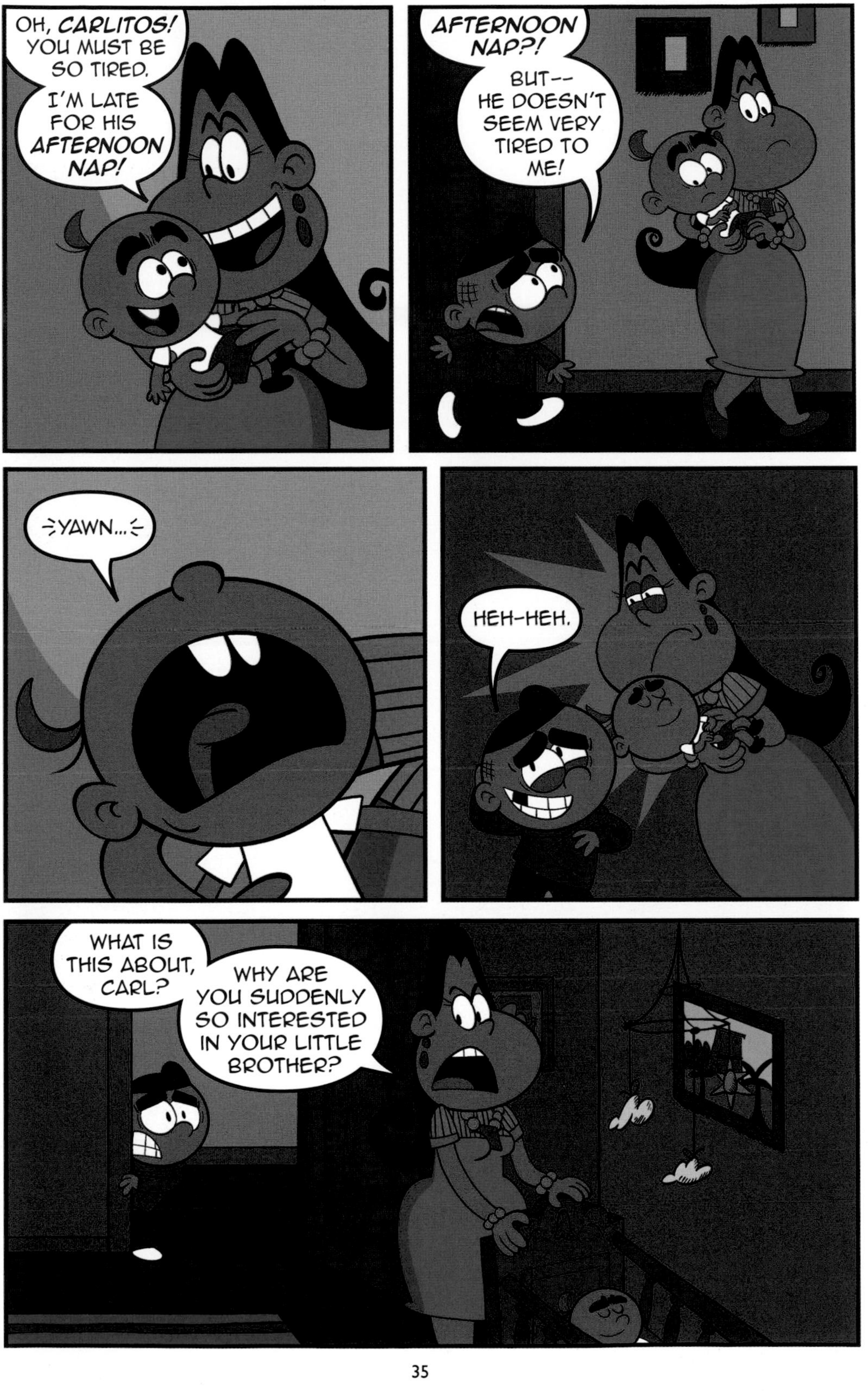
OH, CARLITOS! YOU MUST BE SO TIRED.
I'M LATE FOR HIS AFTERNOON NAP!
AFTERNOON NAP?!
BUT-- HE DOESN'T SEEM VERY TIRED TO ME!
YAWN...
HEH-HEH.
WHAT IS THIS ABOUT, CARL?
WHY ARE YOU SUDDENLY SO INTERESTED IN YOUR LITTLE BROTHER?

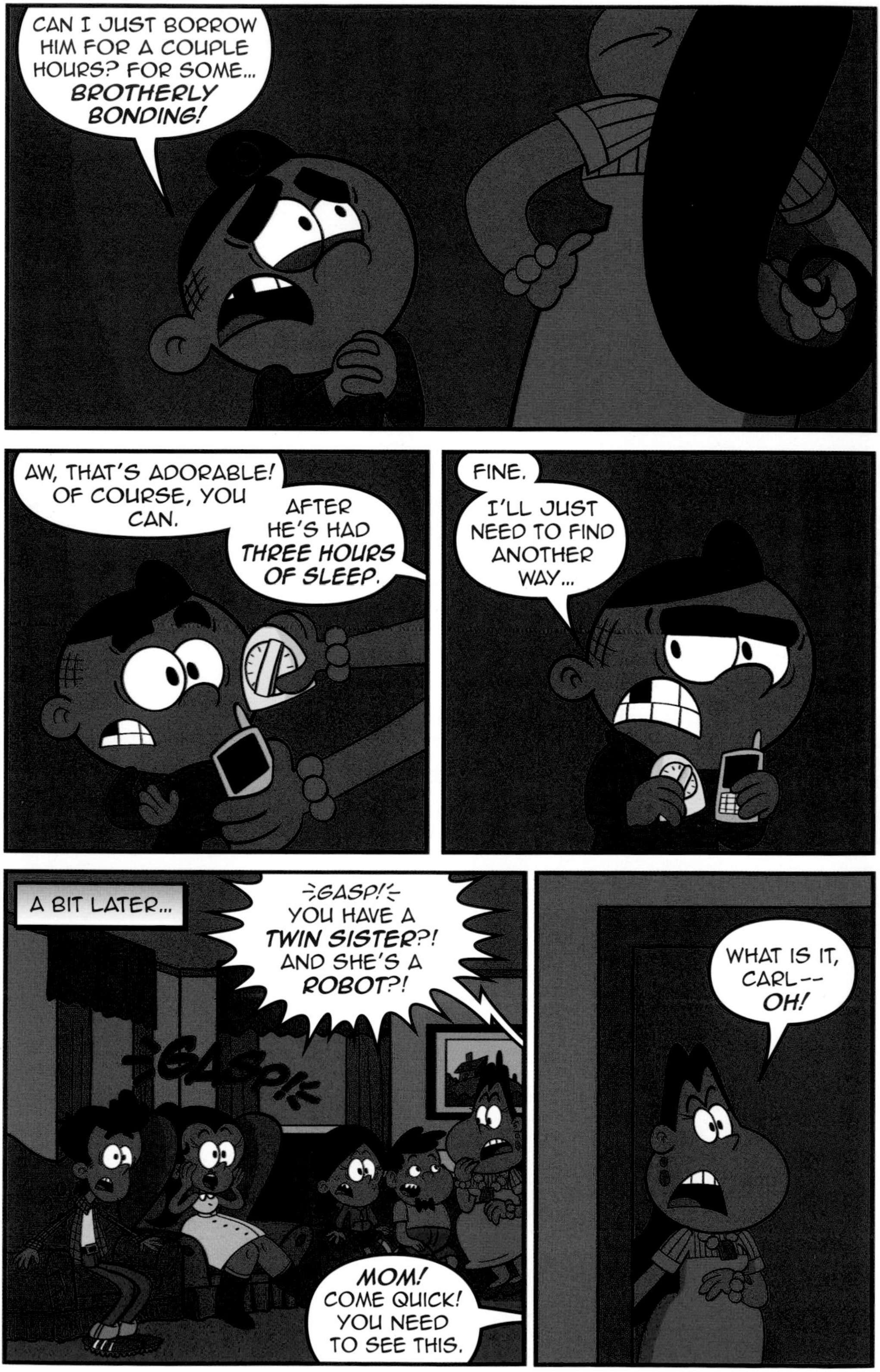
CAN I JUST BORROW HIM FOR A COUPLE HOURS? FOR SOME... BROTHERLY BONDING!
AW, THAT'S ADORABLE! OF COURSE, YOU CAN.
AFTER HE'S HAD THREE HOURS OF SLEEP.
FINE.
I'LL JUST NEED TO FIND ANOTHER WAY...
A BIT LATER...
GASP!
YOU HAVE A TWIN SISTER?! AND SHE'S A ROBOT?!
GASP!
MOM! COME QUICK! YOU NEED TO SEE THIS.
WHAT IS IT, CARL-- OH!

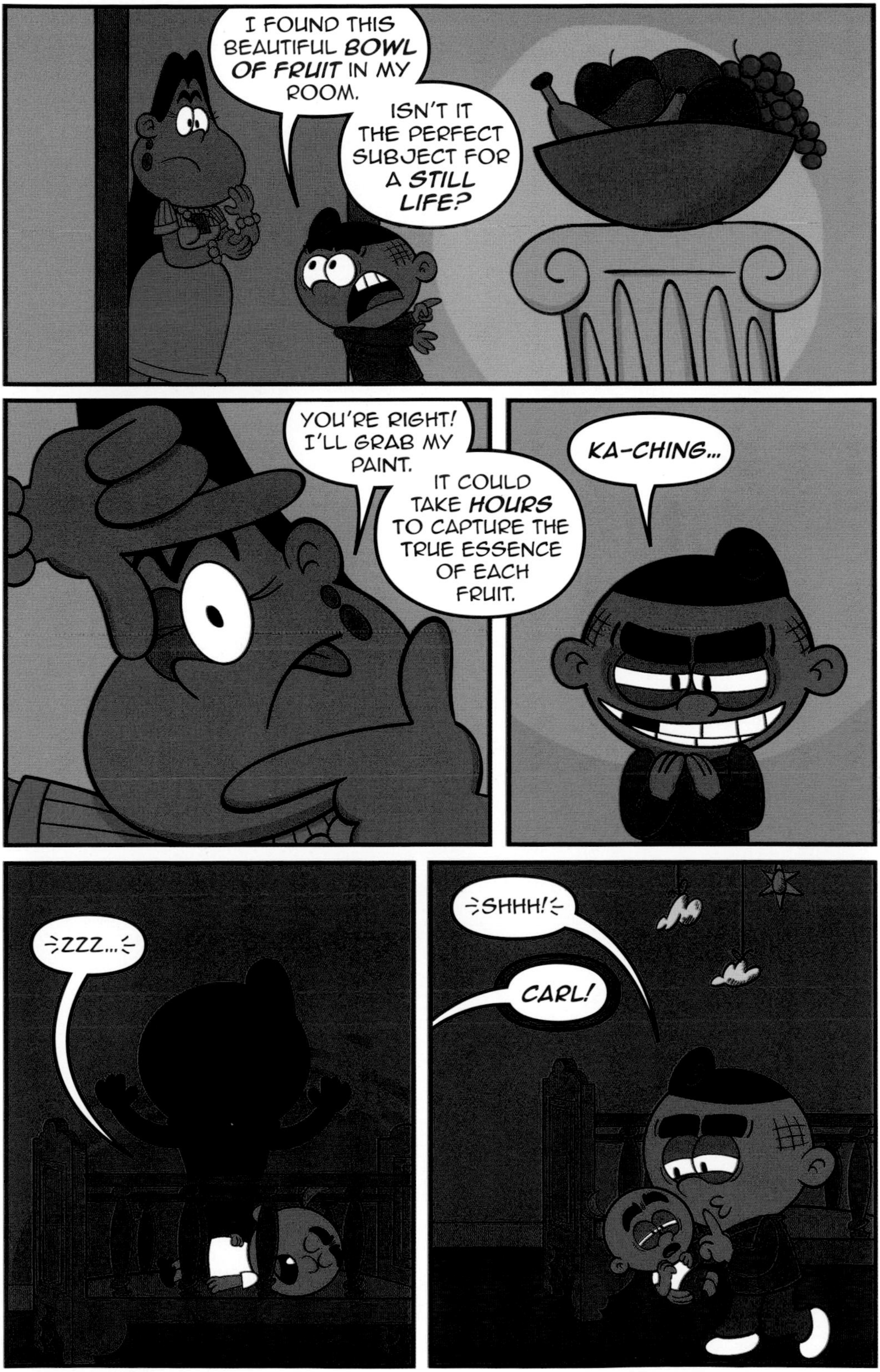
I FOUND THIS BEAUTIFUL BOWL OF FRUIT IN MY ROOM.
ISN'T IT THE PERFECT SUBJECT FOR A STILL LIFE?
YOU'RE RIGHT! I'LL GRAB MY PAINT.
IT COULD TAKE HOURS TO CAPTURE THE TRUE ESSENCE OF EACH FRUIT.
KA-CHING...
ZZZ...
SHHH!
CARL!

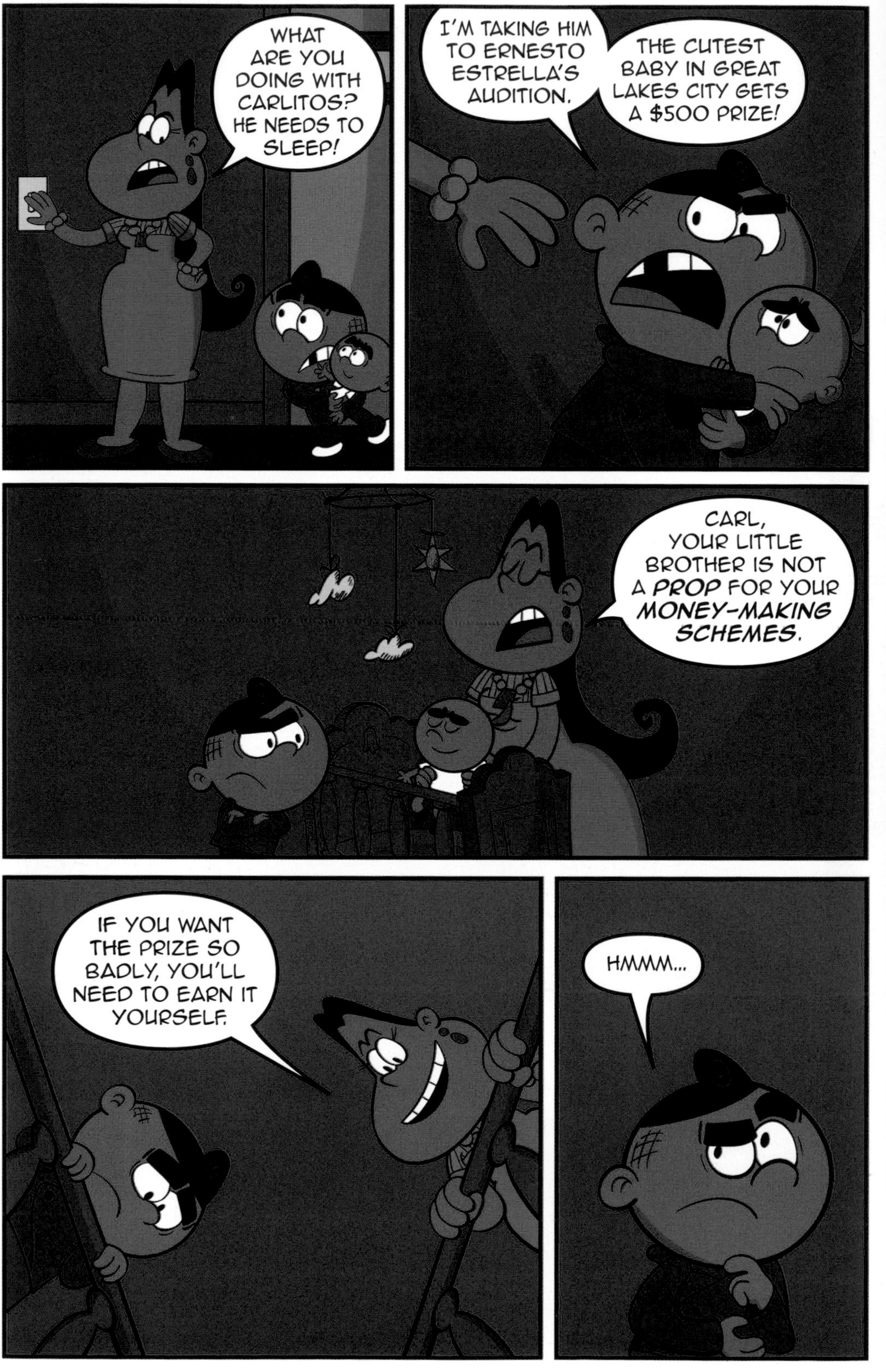
WHAT ARE YOU DOING WITH CARLITOS? HE NEEDS TO SLEEP!
I'M TAKING HIM TO ERNESTO ESTRELLA'S AUDITION.
THE CUTEST BABY IN GREAT LAKES CITY GETS A $500 PRIZE!
CARL, YOUR LITTLE BROTHER IS NOT A *PROP* FOR YOUR ***MONEY-MAKING SCHEMES***.
IF YOU WANT THE PRIZE SO BADLY, YOU'LL NEED TO EARN IT YOURSELF.
HMMM...

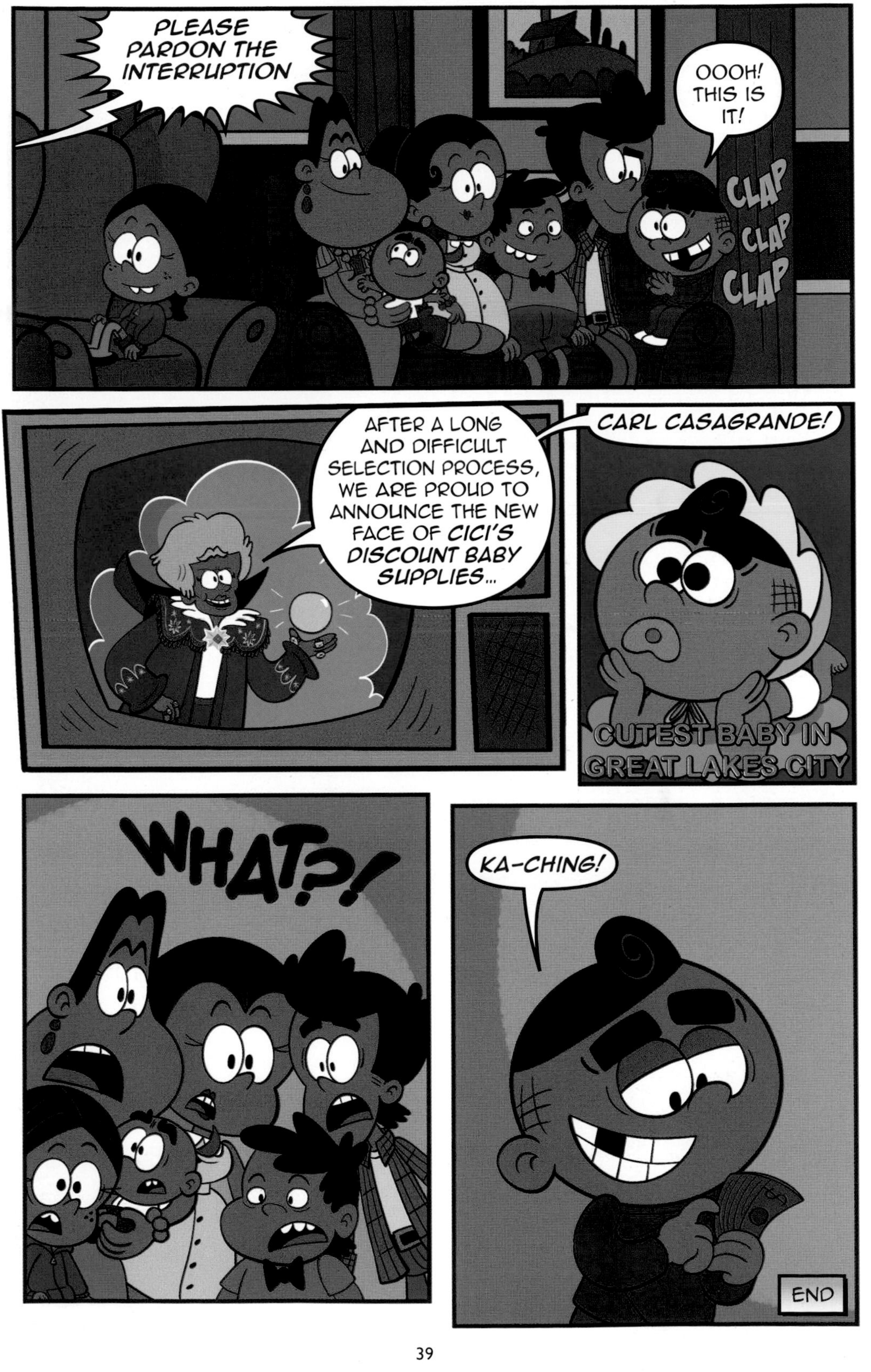
PLEASE PARDON THE INTERRUPTION
OOOH! THIS IS IT!
CLAP CLAP CLAP
AFTER A LONG AND DIFFICULT SELECTION PROCESS, WE ARE PROUD TO ANNOUNCE THE NEW FACE OF CICI'S DISCOUNT BABY SUPPLIES...
CARL CASAGRANDE!
CUTEST BABY IN GREAT LAKES CITY
WHAT?!
KA-CHING!
END

"HALL OF HAUNTS"

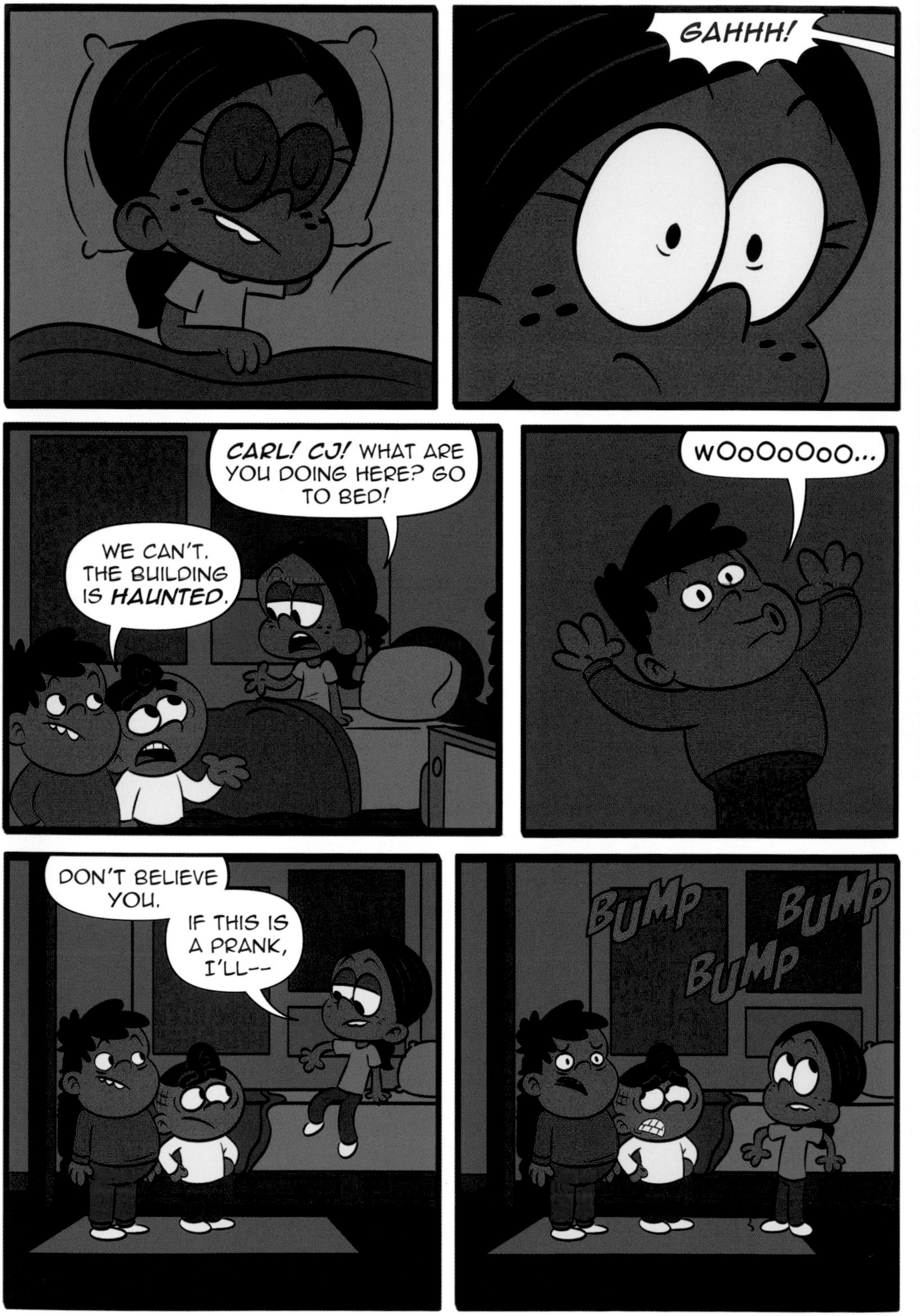

GAHHH!
CARL! CJ! WHAT ARE YOU DOING HERE? GO TO BED!
WE CAN'T. THE BUILDING IS HAUNTED.
WOoOoOoO...
DON'T BELIEVE YOU.
IF THIS IS A PRANK, I'LL--
BUMP
BUMP
BUMP

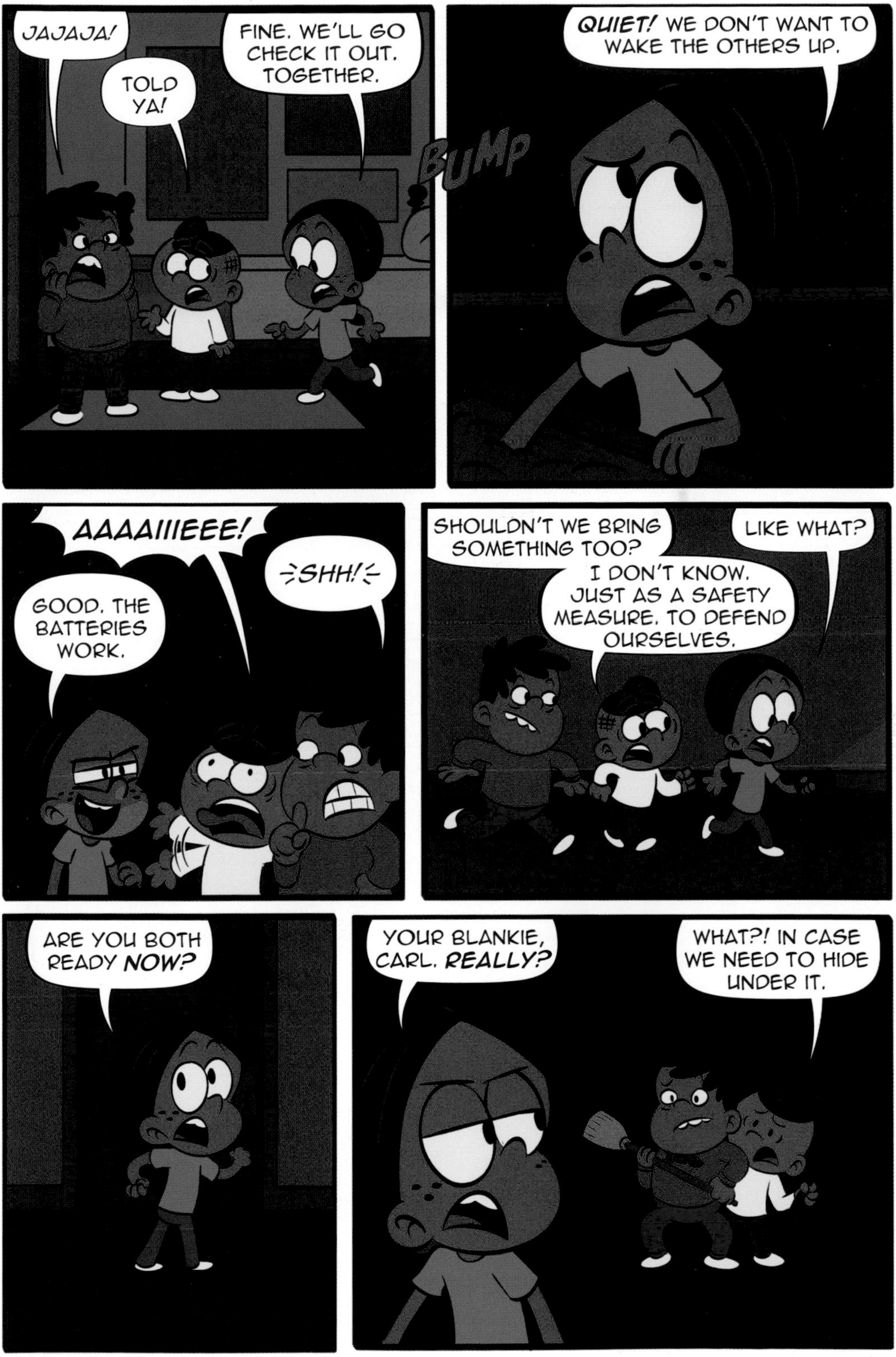
JAJAJA!
TOLD YA!
FINE. WE'LL GO CHECK IT OUT. TOGETHER.
BUMP
QUIET! WE DON'T WANT TO WAKE THE OTHERS UP.
AAAAIIIEEE!
GOOD. THE BATTERIES WORK.
SHH!
SHOULDN'T WE BRING SOMETHING TOO?
LIKE WHAT?
I DON'T KNOW. JUST AS A SAFETY MEASURE. TO DEFEND OURSELVES.
ARE YOU BOTH READY NOW?
YOUR BLANKIE, CARL. REALLY?
WHAT?! IN CASE WE NEED TO HIDE UNDER IT.

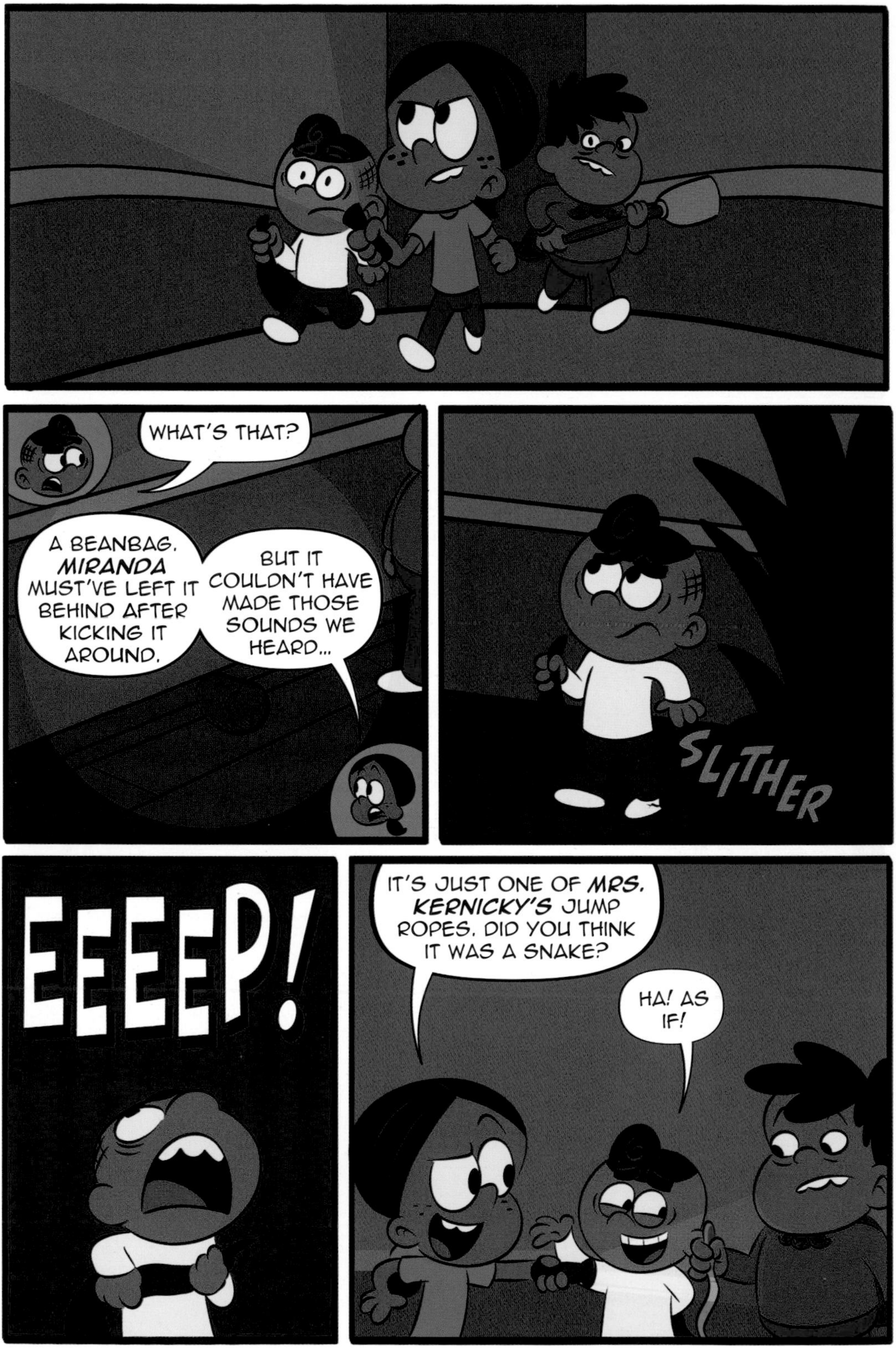
WHAT'S THAT?
A BEANBAG. MIRANDA MUST'VE LEFT IT BEHIND AFTER KICKING IT AROUND.
BUT IT COULDN'T HAVE MADE THOSE SOUNDS WE HEARD...
SLITHER
EEEEP!
IT'S JUST ONE OF MRS. KERNICKY'S JUMP ROPES. DID YOU THINK IT WAS A SNAKE?
HA! AS IF!

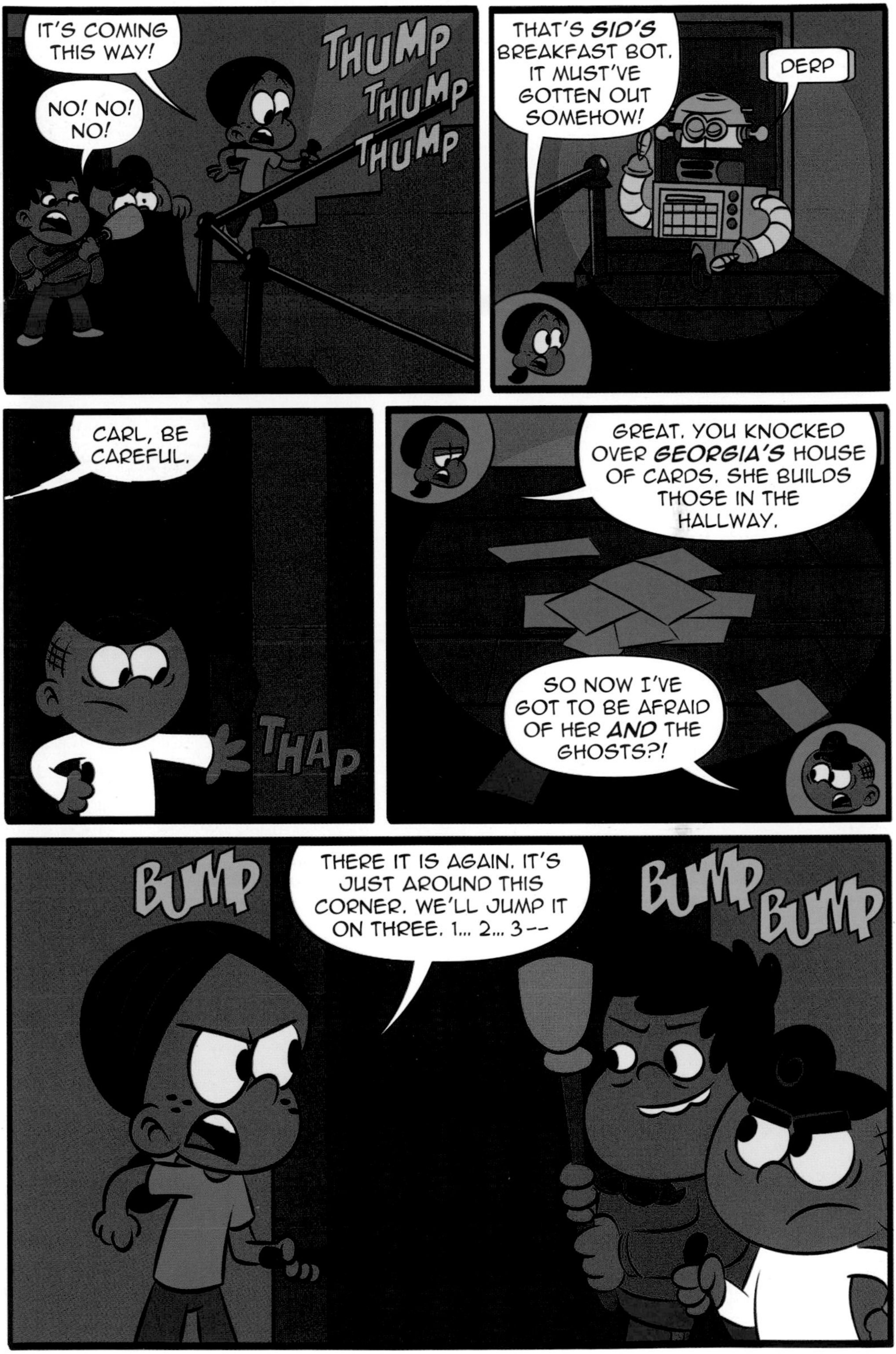
IT'S COMING THIS WAY!
NO! NO! NO!
THUMP THUMP THUMP
THAT'S SID'S BREAKFAST BOT. IT MUST'VE GOTTEN OUT SOMEHOW!
DERP
CARL, BE CAREFUL.
THAP
GREAT. YOU KNOCKED OVER GEORGIA'S HOUSE OF CARDS. SHE BUILDS THOSE IN THE HALLWAY.
SO NOW I'VE GOT TO BE AFRAID OF HER AND THE GHOSTS?!
BUMP
THERE IT IS AGAIN. IT'S JUST AROUND THIS CORNER. WE'LL JUMP IT ON THREE. 1... 2... 3 --
BUMP BUMP

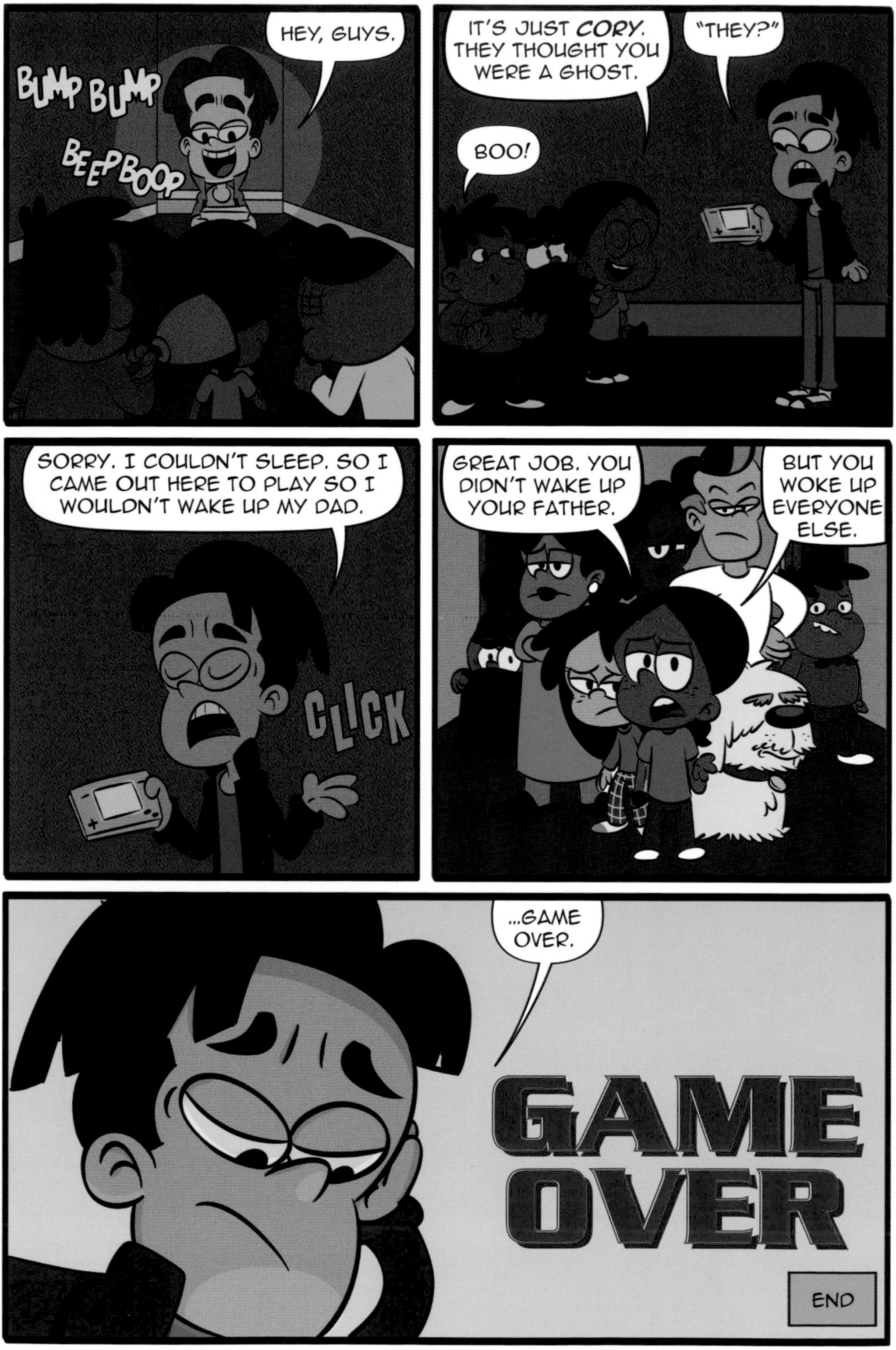
HEY, GUYS.
BUMP BUMP
BEEP BOOP
IT'S JUST *CORY*. THEY THOUGHT YOU WERE A GHOST.
"THEY?"
BOO!
SORRY. I COULDN'T SLEEP. SO I CAME OUT HERE TO PLAY SO I WOULDN'T WAKE UP MY DAD.
CLICK
GREAT JOB. YOU DIDN'T WAKE UP YOUR FATHER.
BUT YOU WOKE UP EVERYONE ELSE.
...GAME OVER.
GAME OVER
END

"BEAR WITH IT"

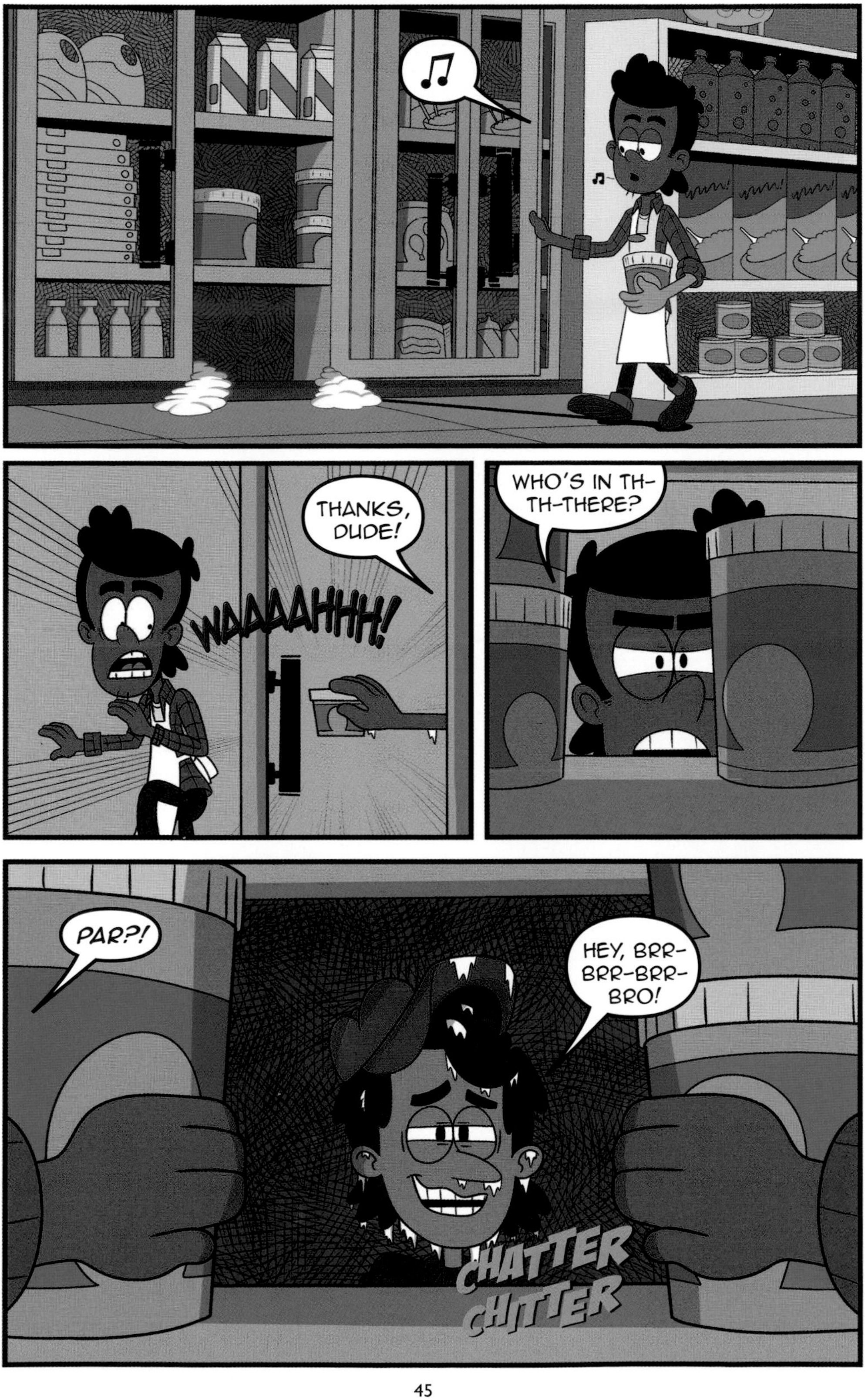
♫
THANKS, DUDE!
WAAAAHHH!
WHO'S IN TH-TH-THERE?
PAR?!
HEY, BRR-BRR-BRR-BRO!
CHATTER
CHITTER

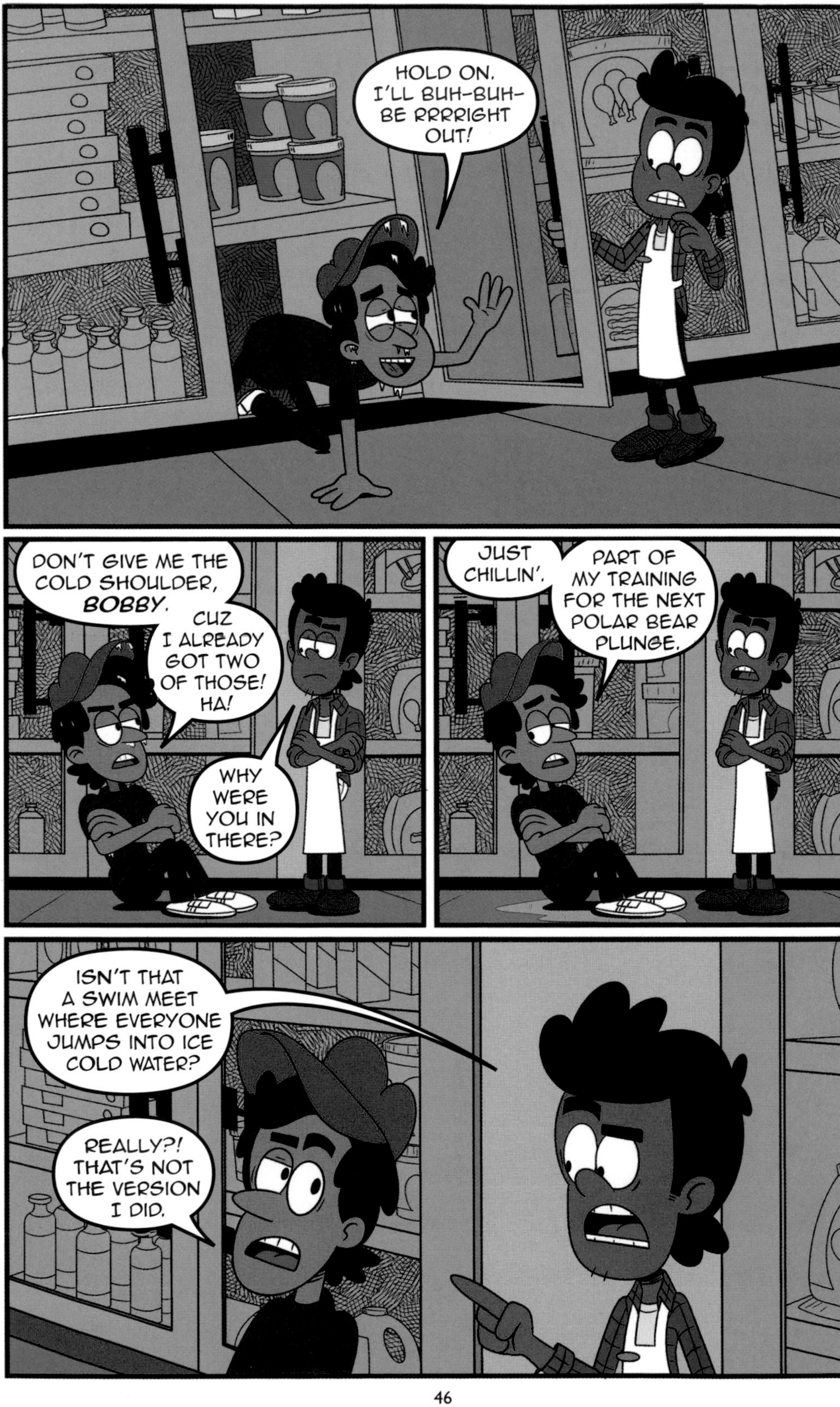
HOLD ON. I'LL BUH-BUH-BE RRRRIGHT OUT!
DON'T GIVE ME THE COLD SHOULDER, BOBBY.
CUZ I ALREADY GOT TWO OF THOSE! HA!
WHY WERE YOU IN THERE?
JUST CHILLIN'.
PART OF MY TRAINING FOR THE NEXT POLAR BEAR PLUNGE.
ISN'T THAT A SWIM MEET WHERE EVERYONE JUMPS INTO ICE COLD WATER?
REALLY?! THAT'S NOT THE VERSION I DID.

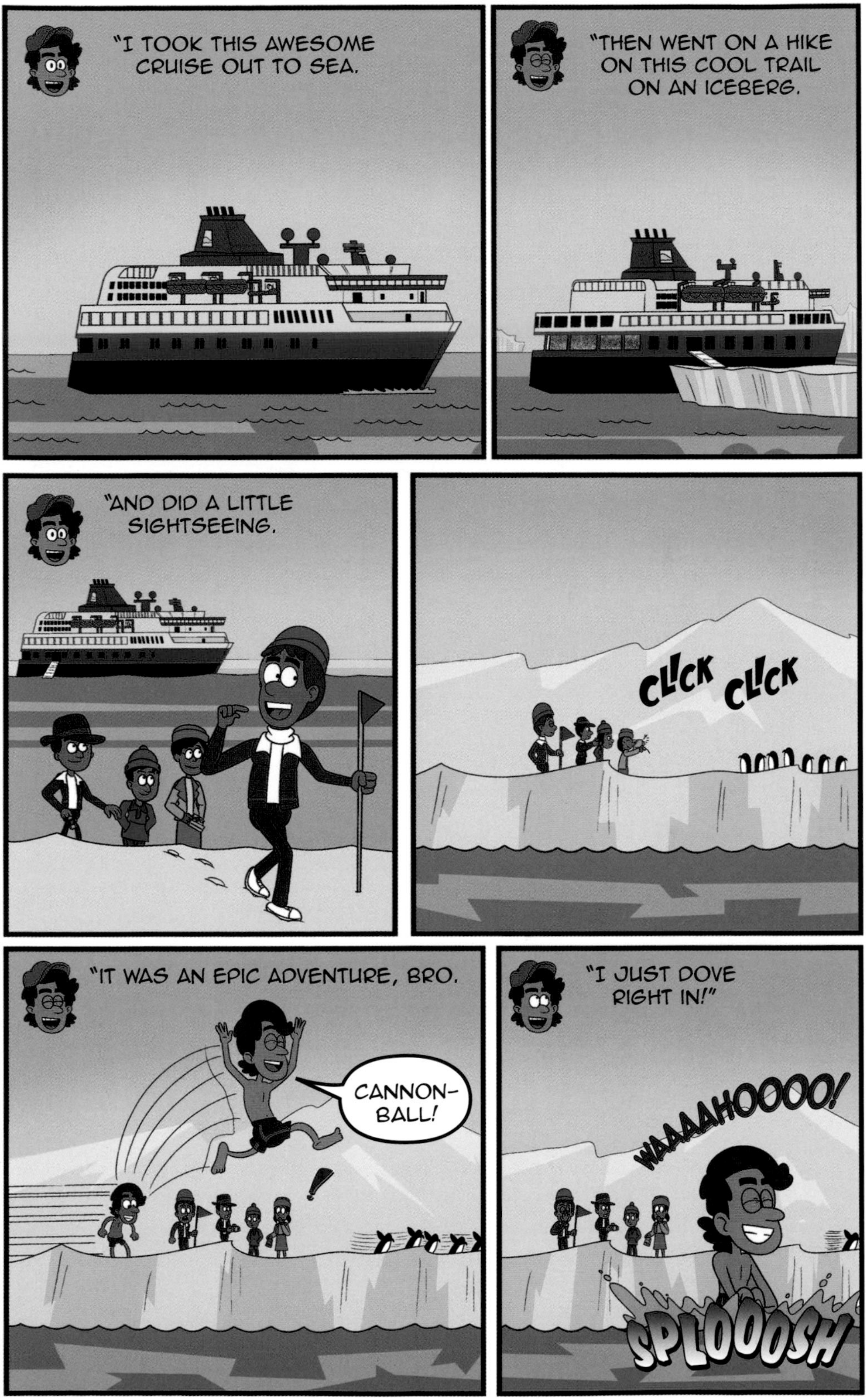
"I TOOK THIS AWESOME CRUISE OUT TO SEA.
"THEN WENT ON A HIKE ON THIS COOL TRAIL ON AN ICEBERG.
"AND DID A LITTLE SIGHTSEEING.
CLICK
CLICK
"IT WAS AN EPIC ADVENTURE, BRO.
CANNON-BALL!
!
"I JUST DOVE RIGHT IN!"
WAAAAHOOOOO!
SPLOOOSH

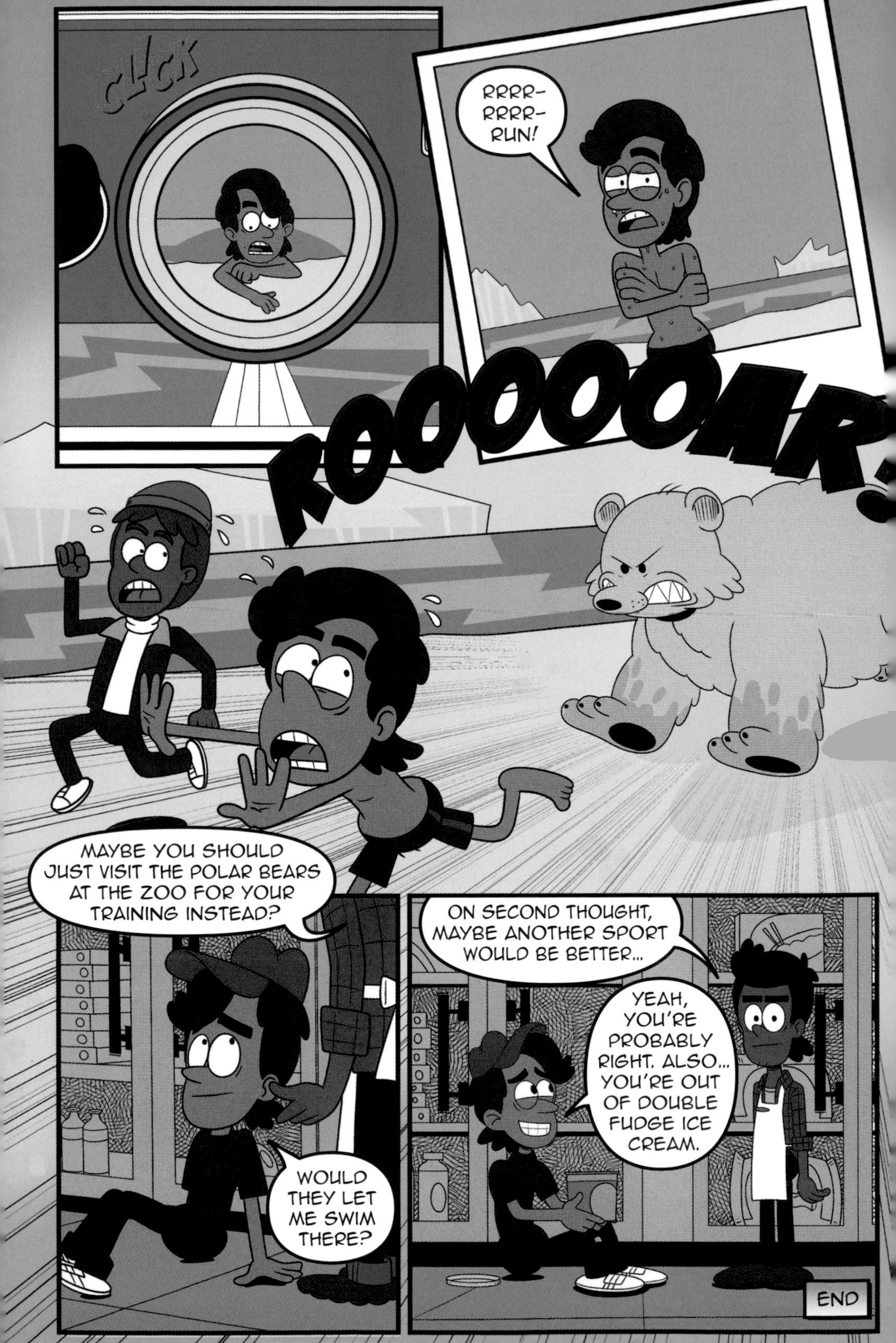
CLICK
RRRR-
RRRR-
RUN!
ROOOOOAR!
MAYBE YOU SHOULD JUST VISIT THE POLAR BEARS AT THE ZOO FOR YOUR TRAINING INSTEAD?
WOULD THEY LET ME SWIM THERE?
ON SECOND THOUGHT, MAYBE ANOTHER SPORT WOULD BE BETTER...
YEAH, YOU'RE PROBABLY RIGHT. ALSO... YOU'RE OUT OF DOUBLE FUDGE ICE CREAM.
END

"THE NIGHT MERCADO"

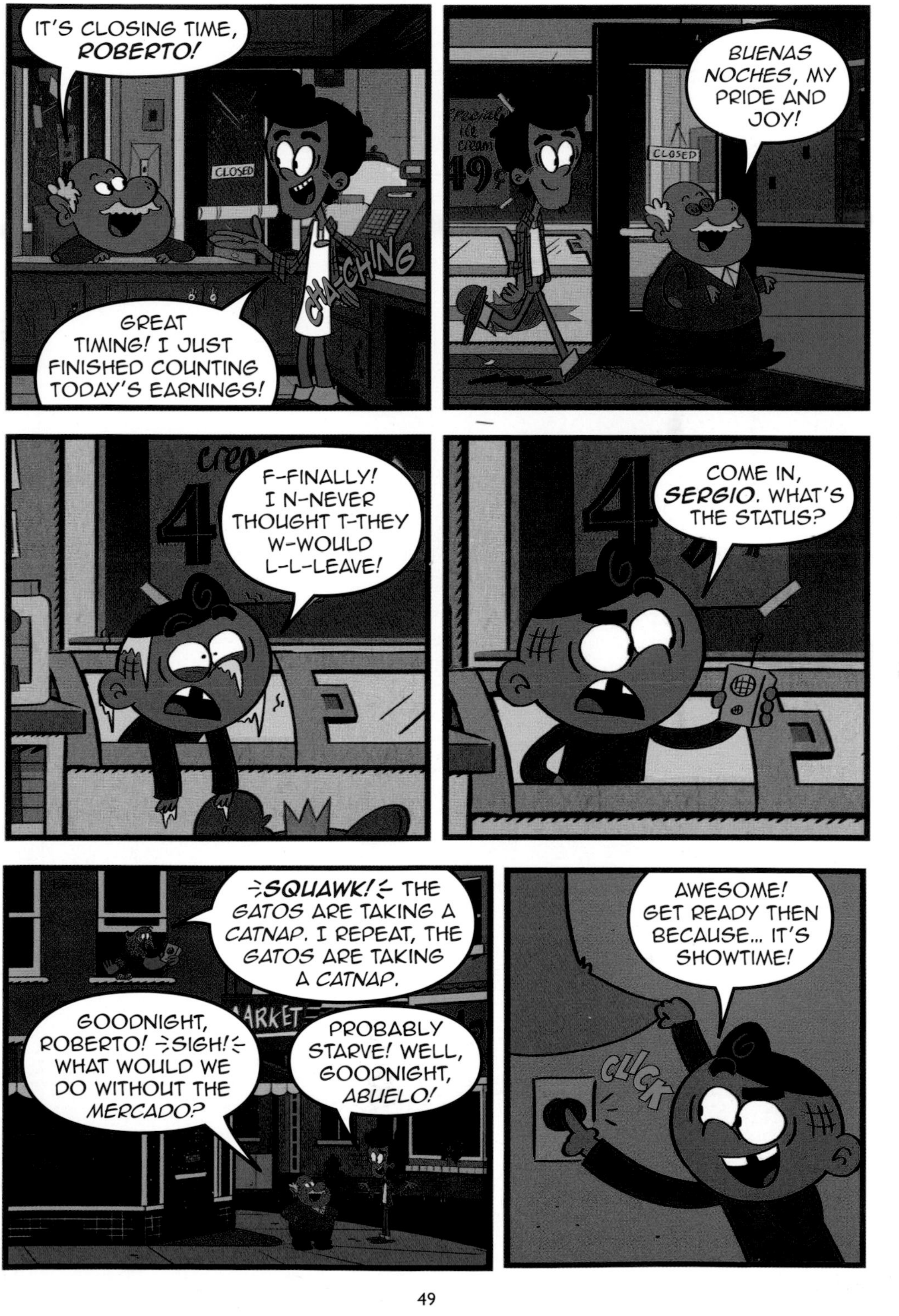

IT'S CLOSING TIME, ROBERTO!
GREAT TIMING! I JUST FINISHED COUNTING TODAY'S EARNINGS!
CHA-CHING
CLOSED
BUENAS NOCHES, MY PRIDE AND JOY!
CLOSED
F-FINALLY! I N-NEVER THOUGHT T-THEY W-WOULD L-L-LEAVE!
COME IN, SERGIO. WHAT'S THE STATUS?
SQUAWK! THE GATOS ARE TAKING A CATNAP. I REPEAT, THE GATOS ARE TAKING A CATNAP.
GOODNIGHT, ROBERTO! SIGH! WHAT WOULD WE DO WITHOUT THE MERCADO?
PROBABLY STARVE! WELL, GOODNIGHT, ABUELO!
AWESOME! GET READY THEN BECAUSE... IT'S SHOWTIME!
CLICK

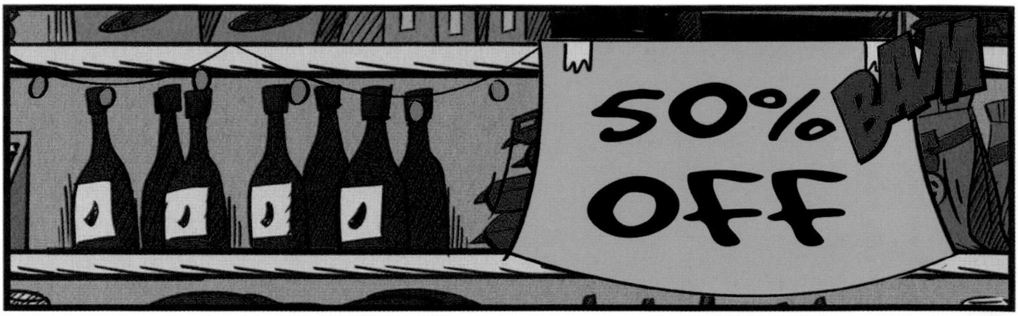
50% OFF
BAM

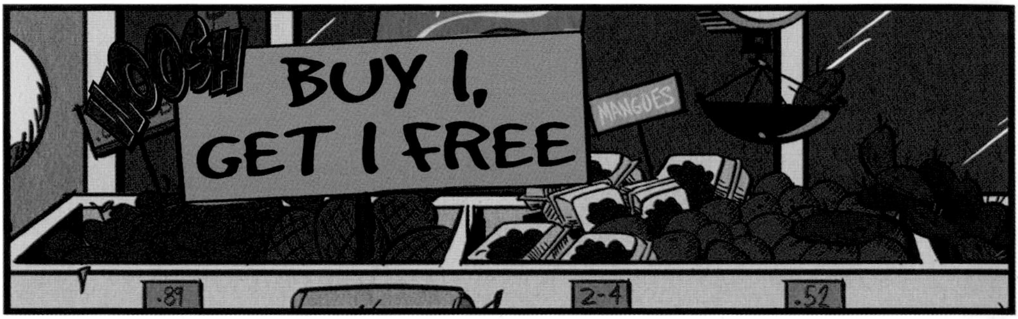
WOOSH
BUY 1, GET 1 FREE
MANGUES
.89
2-4
.52

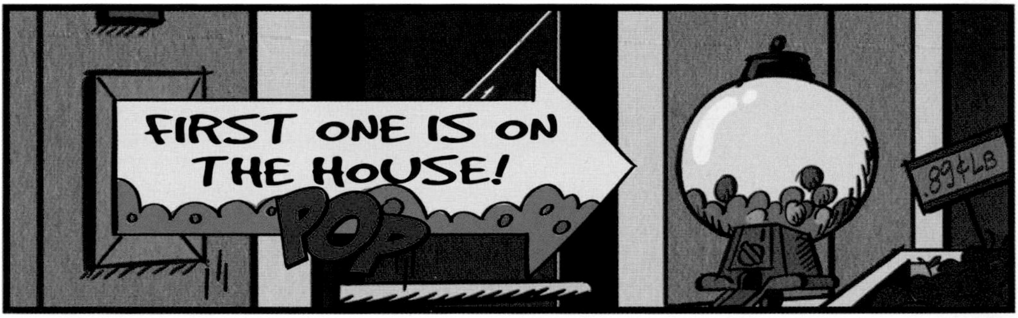
FIRST ONE IS ON THE HOUSE!
POP
.89¢LB

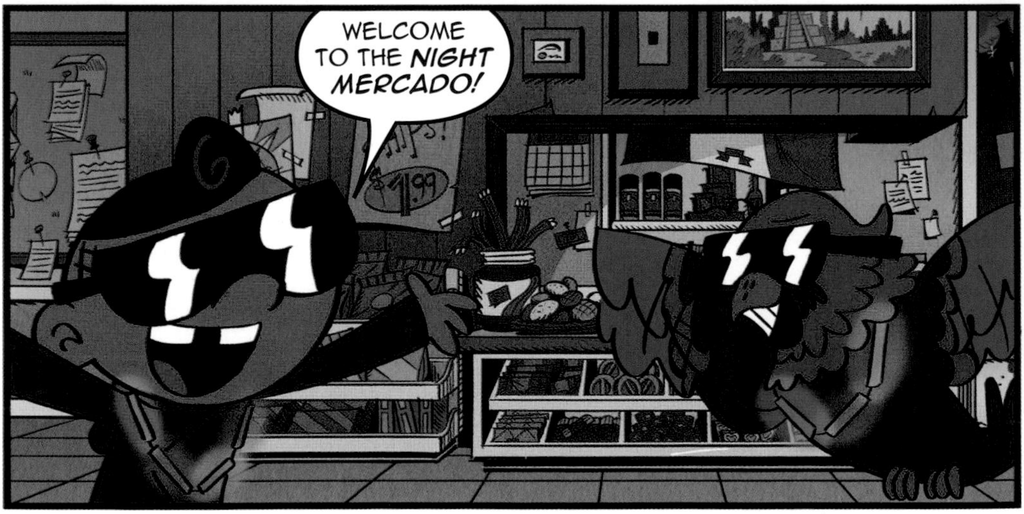
WELCOME TO THE *NIGHT MERCADO!*
$1.99

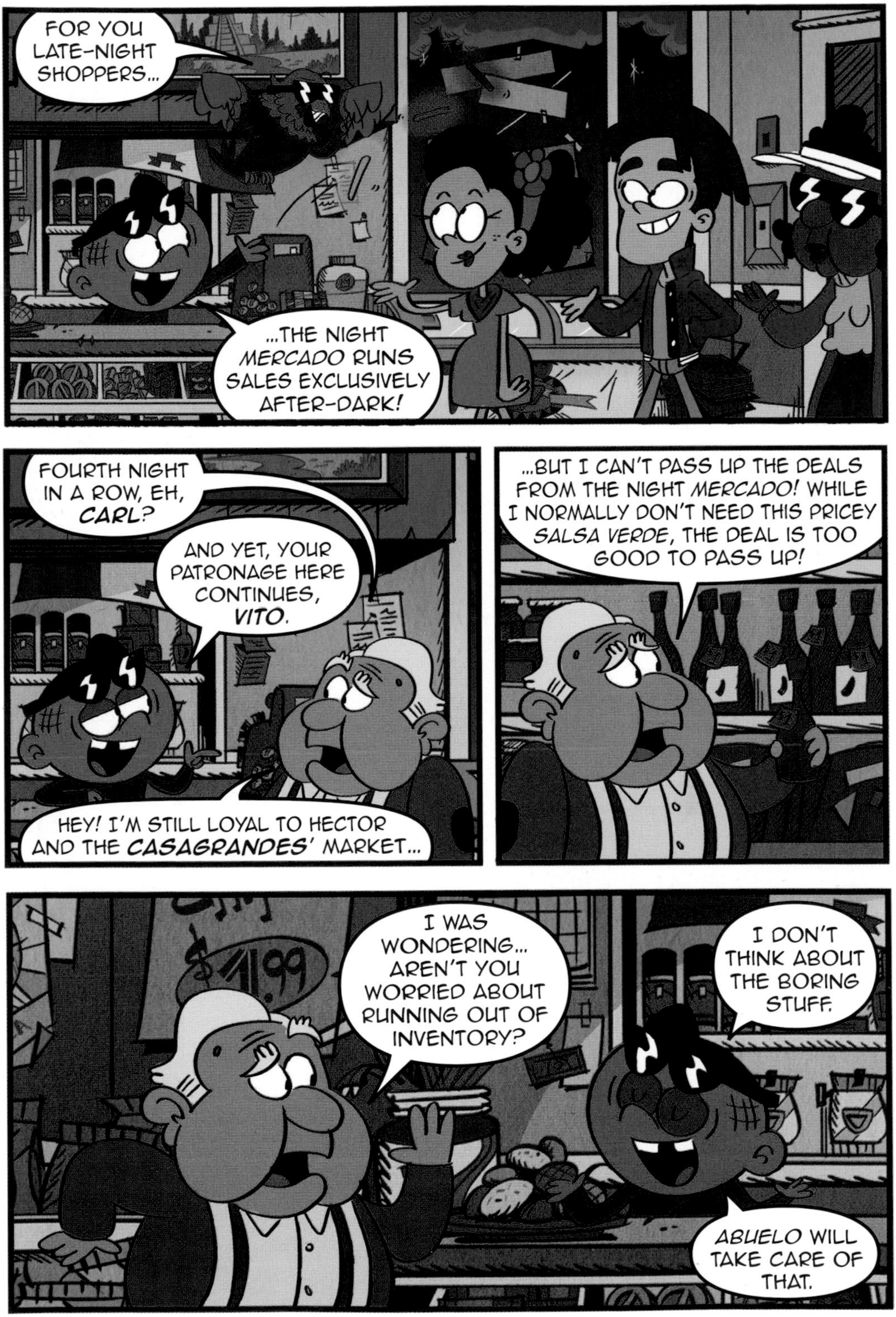
FOR YOU LATE-NIGHT SHOPPERS...
...THE NIGHT *MERCADO* RUNS SALES EXCLUSIVELY AFTER-DARK!
FOURTH NIGHT IN A ROW, EH, **CARL**?
AND YET, YOUR PATRONAGE HERE CONTINUES, **VITO**.
HEY! I'M STILL LOYAL TO HECTOR AND THE **CASAGRANDES'** MARKET...
...BUT I CAN'T PASS UP THE DEALS FROM THE NIGHT *MERCADO*! WHILE I NORMALLY DON'T NEED THIS PRICEY *SALSA VERDE*, THE DEAL IS TOO GOOD TO PASS UP!
$1.99
I WAS WONDERING... AREN'T YOU WORRIED ABOUT RUNNING OUT OF INVENTORY?
I DON'T THINK ABOUT THE BORING STUFF.
ABUELO WILL TAKE CARE OF THAT.

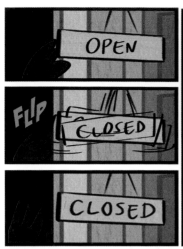

OPEN

FLIP

CLOSED

CLOSED

AS GOOD AS NEW.

WOO!

≳SHHH!≲

WOOSH

Z Z Z Z Z

LATER THAT MORNING...

HMM... THAT DOESN'T ADD UP...

5 bottles

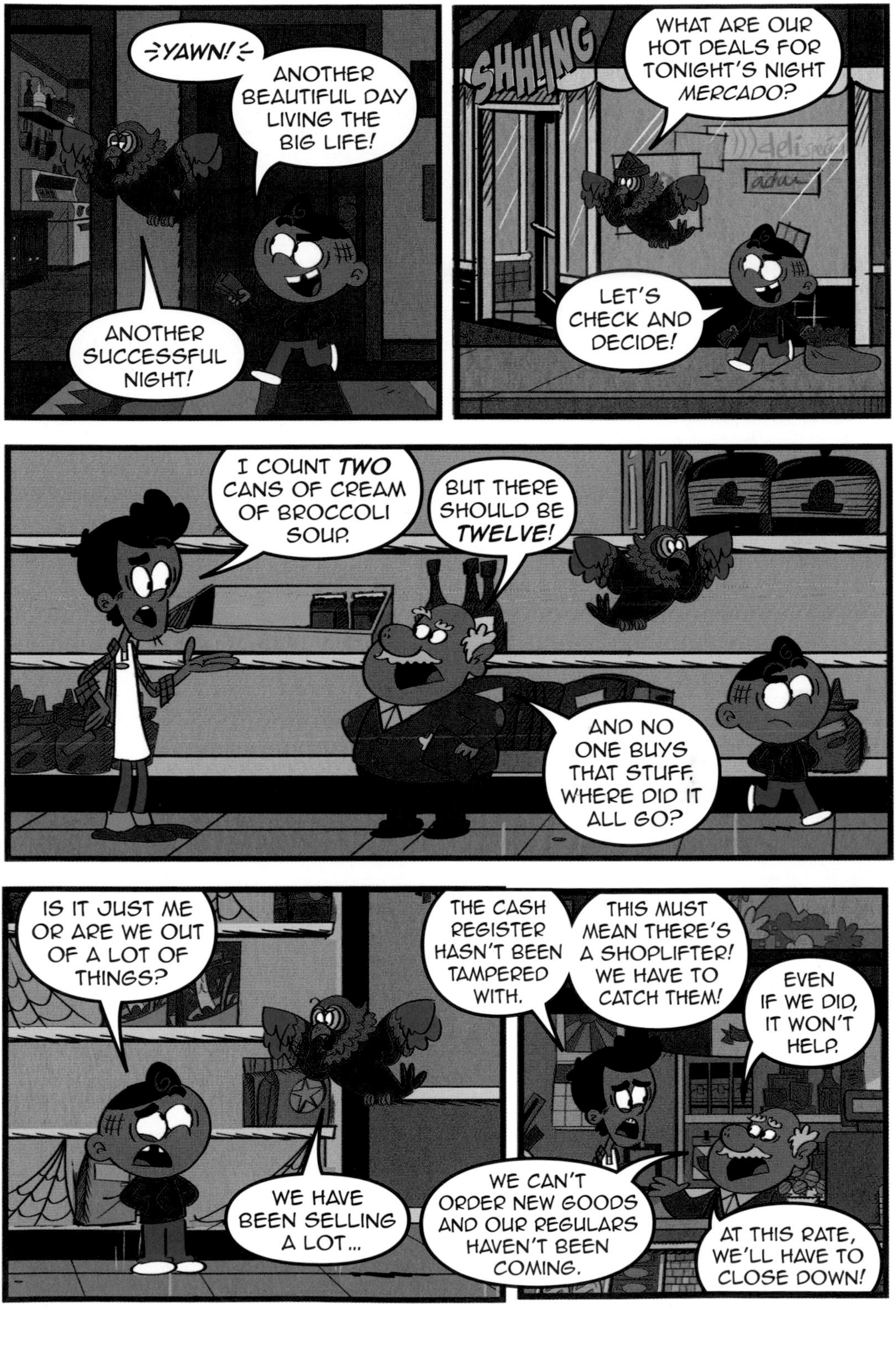

YAWN!
ANOTHER BEAUTIFUL DAY LIVING THE BIG LIFE!
ANOTHER SUCCESSFUL NIGHT!
SHHLING
WHAT ARE OUR HOT DEALS FOR TONIGHT'S NIGHT MERCADO?
LET'S CHECK AND DECIDE!
I COUNT TWO CANS OF CREAM OF BROCCOLI SOUP.
BUT THERE SHOULD BE TWELVE!
AND NO ONE BUYS THAT STUFF. WHERE DID IT ALL GO?
IS IT JUST ME OR ARE WE OUT OF A LOT OF THINGS?
WE HAVE BEEN SELLING A LOT...
THE CASH REGISTER HASN'T BEEN TAMPERED WITH.
THIS MUST MEAN THERE'S A SHOPLIFTER! WE HAVE TO CATCH THEM!
EVEN IF WE DID, IT WON'T HELP.
WE CAN'T ORDER NEW GOODS AND OUR REGULARS HAVEN'T BEEN COMING.
AT THIS RATE, WE'LL HAVE TO CLOSE DOWN!

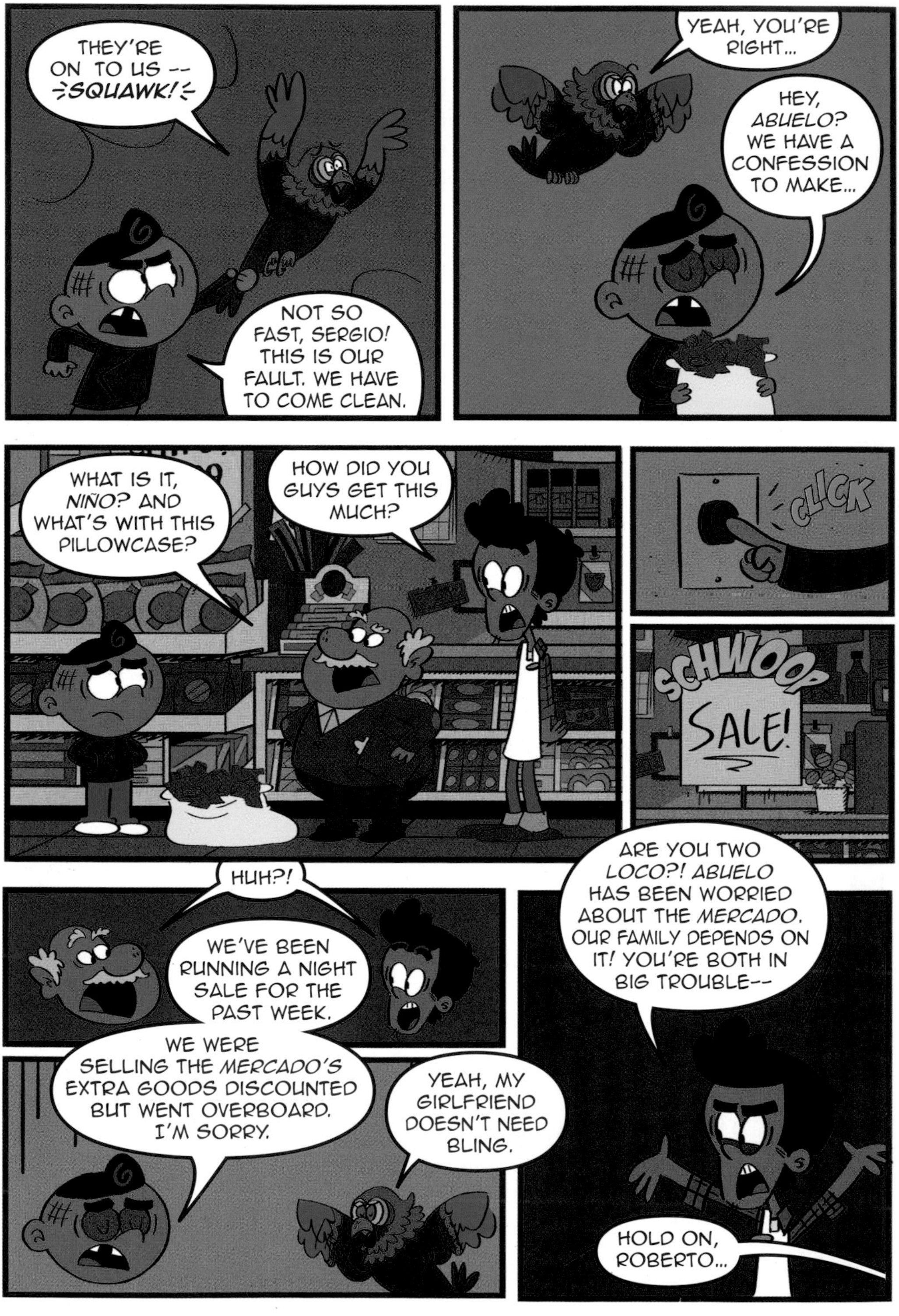
THEY'RE ON TO US -- SQUAWK!
NOT SO FAST, SERGIO! THIS IS OUR FAULT. WE HAVE TO COME CLEAN.
YEAH, YOU'RE RIGHT...
HEY, ABUELO? WE HAVE A CONFESSION TO MAKE...
WHAT IS IT, NIÑO? AND WHAT'S WITH THIS PILLOWCASE?
HOW DID YOU GUYS GET THIS MUCH?
CLICK
SCHWOOP
SALE!
HUH?!
WE'VE BEEN RUNNING A NIGHT SALE FOR THE PAST WEEK.
WE WERE SELLING THE MERCADO'S EXTRA GOODS DISCOUNTED BUT WENT OVERBOARD. I'M SORRY.
YEAH, MY GIRLFRIEND DOESN'T NEED BLING.
ARE YOU TWO LOCO?! ABUELO HAS BEEN WORRIED ABOUT THE MERCADO. OUR FAMILY DEPENDS ON IT! YOU'RE BOTH IN BIG TROUBLE--
HOLD ON, ROBERTO...

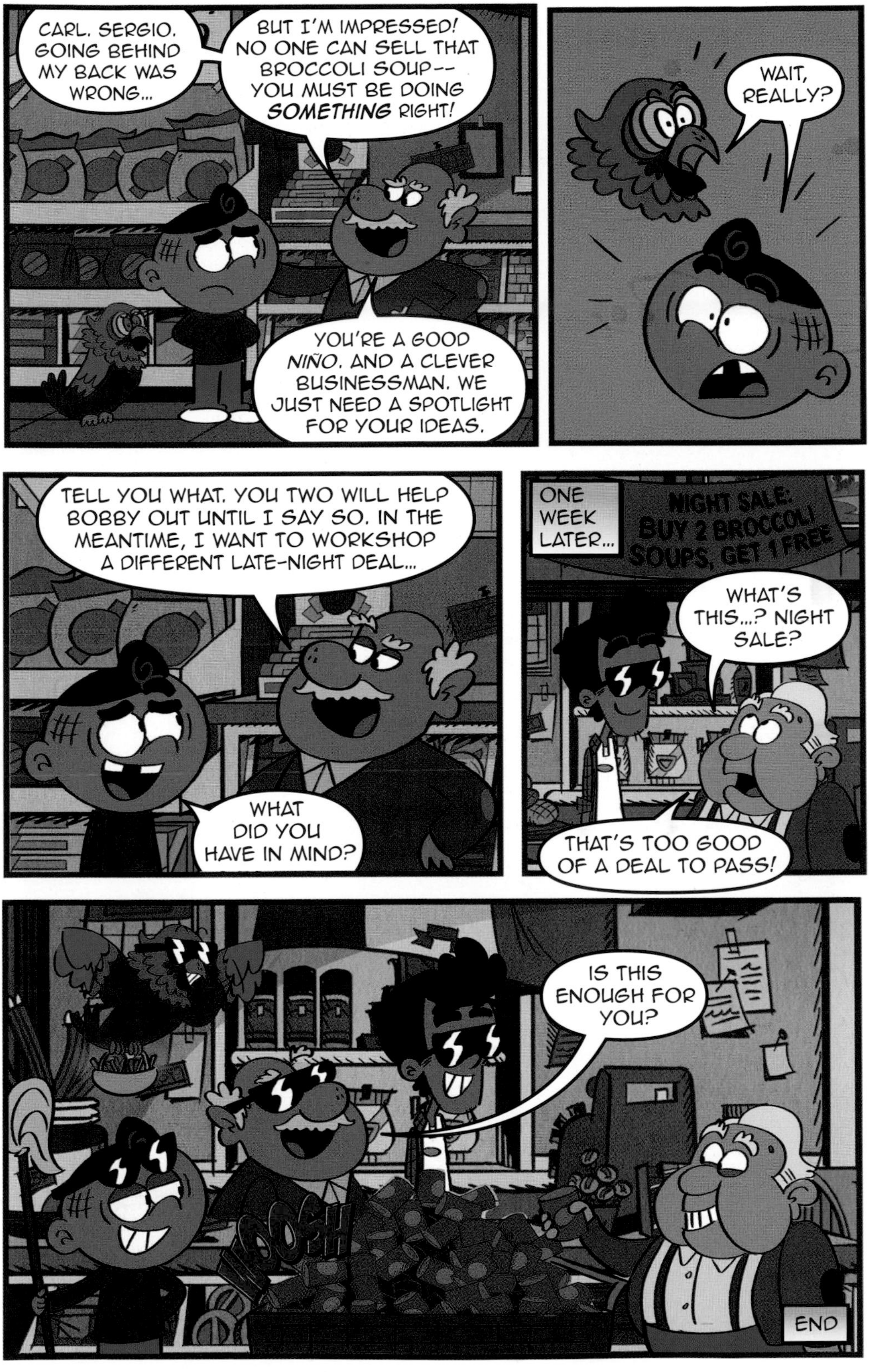
CARL. SERGIO. GOING BEHIND MY BACK WAS WRONG...
BUT I'M IMPRESSED! NO ONE CAN SELL THAT BROCCOLI SOUP-- YOU MUST BE DOING *SOMETHING* RIGHT!
YOU'RE A GOOD *NIÑO*. AND A CLEVER BUSINESSMAN. WE JUST NEED A SPOTLIGHT FOR YOUR IDEAS.
WAIT, REALLY?
TELL YOU WHAT. YOU TWO WILL HELP BOBBY OUT UNTIL I SAY SO. IN THE MEANTIME, I WANT TO WORKSHOP A DIFFERENT LATE-NIGHT DEAL...
WHAT DID YOU HAVE IN MIND?
ONE WEEK LATER...
NIGHT SALE: BUY 2 BROCCOLI SOUPS, GET 1 FREE
WHAT'S THIS...? NIGHT SALE?
THAT'S TOO GOOD OF A DEAL TO PASS!
IS THIS ENOUGH FOR YOU?
END

"ALONE TIME"

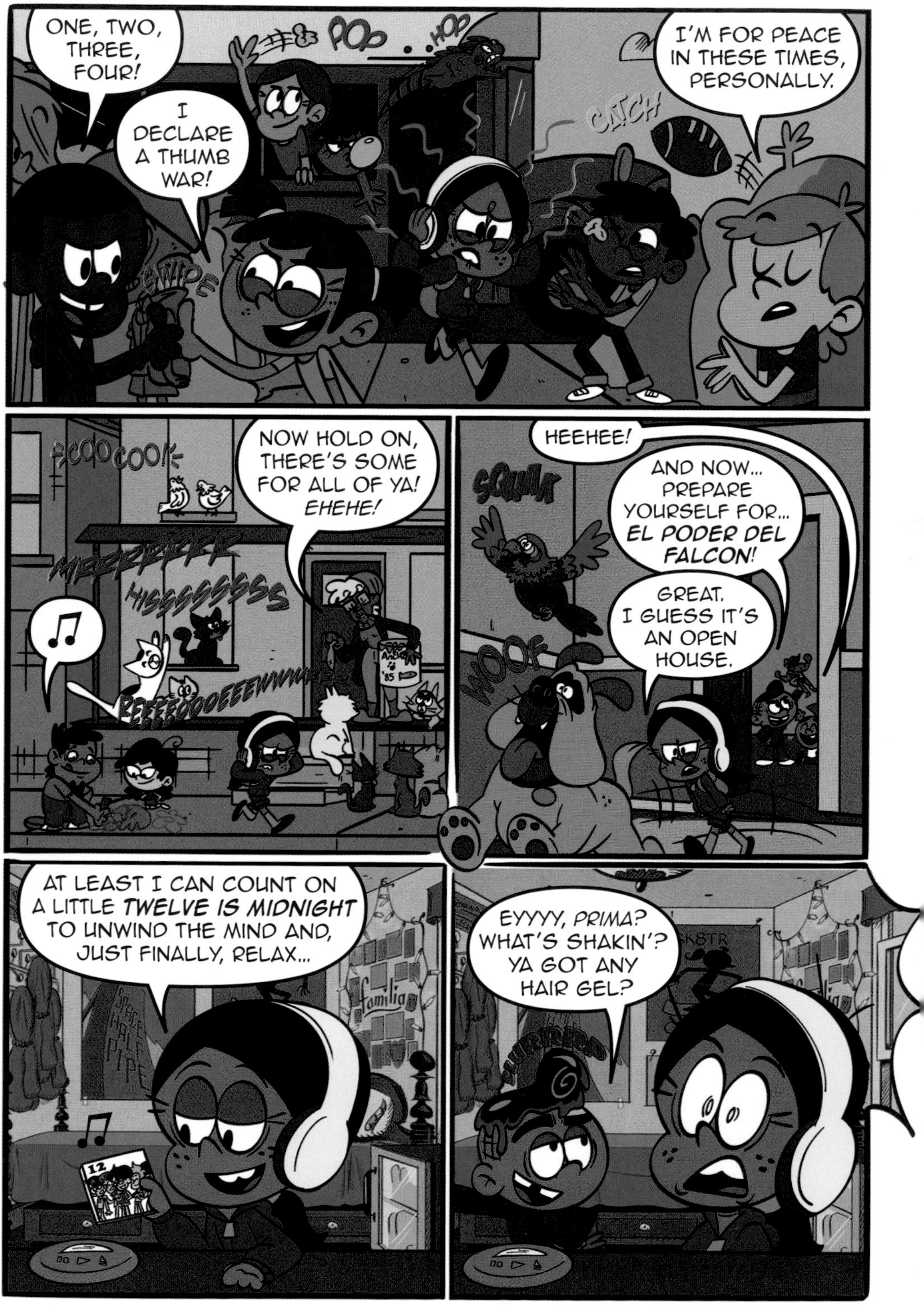

ONE, TWO, THREE, FOUR!
I DECLARE A THUMB WAR!
POP
HOP
CATCH
I'M FOR PEACE IN THESE TIMES, PERSONALLY.
SWIPE
COO COO
NOW HOLD ON, THERE'S SOME FOR ALL OF YA! *EHEHE!*
MRRRRRRR
HISSSSSSSS
♫
HEEHEE!
SQUAK
AND NOW... PREPARE YOURSELF FOR... ***EL PODER DEL FALCON***!
GREAT. I GUESS IT'S AN OPEN HOUSE.
WOOF
AT LEAST I CAN COUNT ON A LITTLE ***TWELVE IS MIDNIGHT*** TO UNWIND THE MIND AND, JUST FINALLY, RELAX...
familia
EYYYY, *PRIMA*? WHAT'S SHAKIN'? YA GOT ANY HAIR GEL?

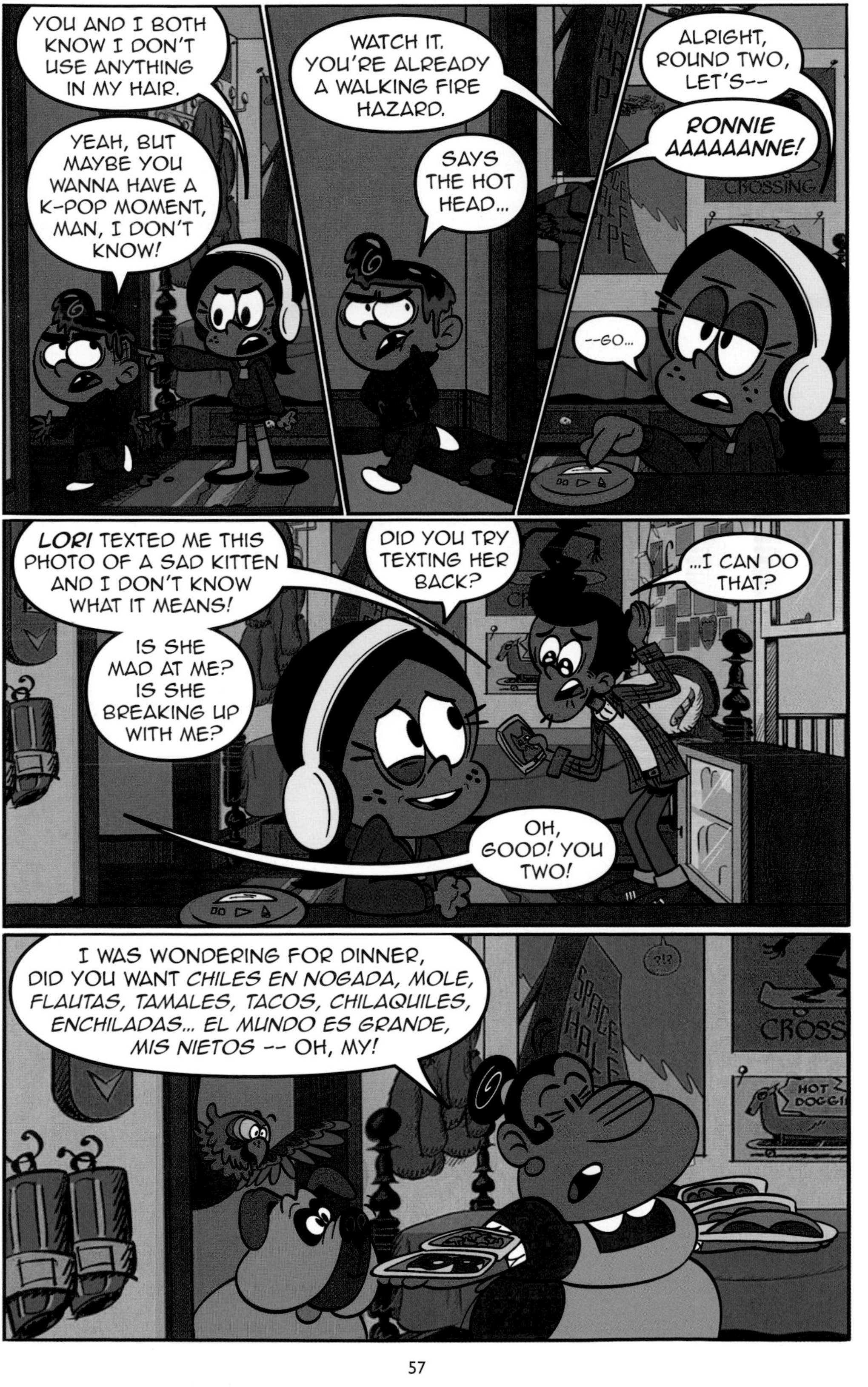
YOU AND I BOTH KNOW I DON'T USE ANYTHING IN MY HAIR.
YEAH, BUT MAYBE YOU WANNA HAVE A K-POP MOMENT, MAN, I DON'T KNOW!
WATCH IT. YOU'RE ALREADY A WALKING FIRE HAZARD.
SAYS THE HOT HEAD...
ALRIGHT, ROUND TWO, LET'S--
RONNIE AAAAAAANNE!
--GO...
LORI TEXTED ME THIS PHOTO OF A SAD KITTEN AND I DON'T KNOW WHAT IT MEANS!
IS SHE MAD AT ME? IS SHE BREAKING UP WITH ME?
DID YOU TRY TEXTING HER BACK?
...I CAN DO THAT?
OH, GOOD! YOU TWO!
I WAS WONDERING FOR DINNER, DID YOU WANT CHILES EN NOGADA, MOLE, FLAUTAS, TAMALES, TACOS, CHILAQUILES, ENCHILADAS... EL MUNDO ES GRANDE, MIS NIETOS -- OH, MY!
CROSSING
HOT DOGGI

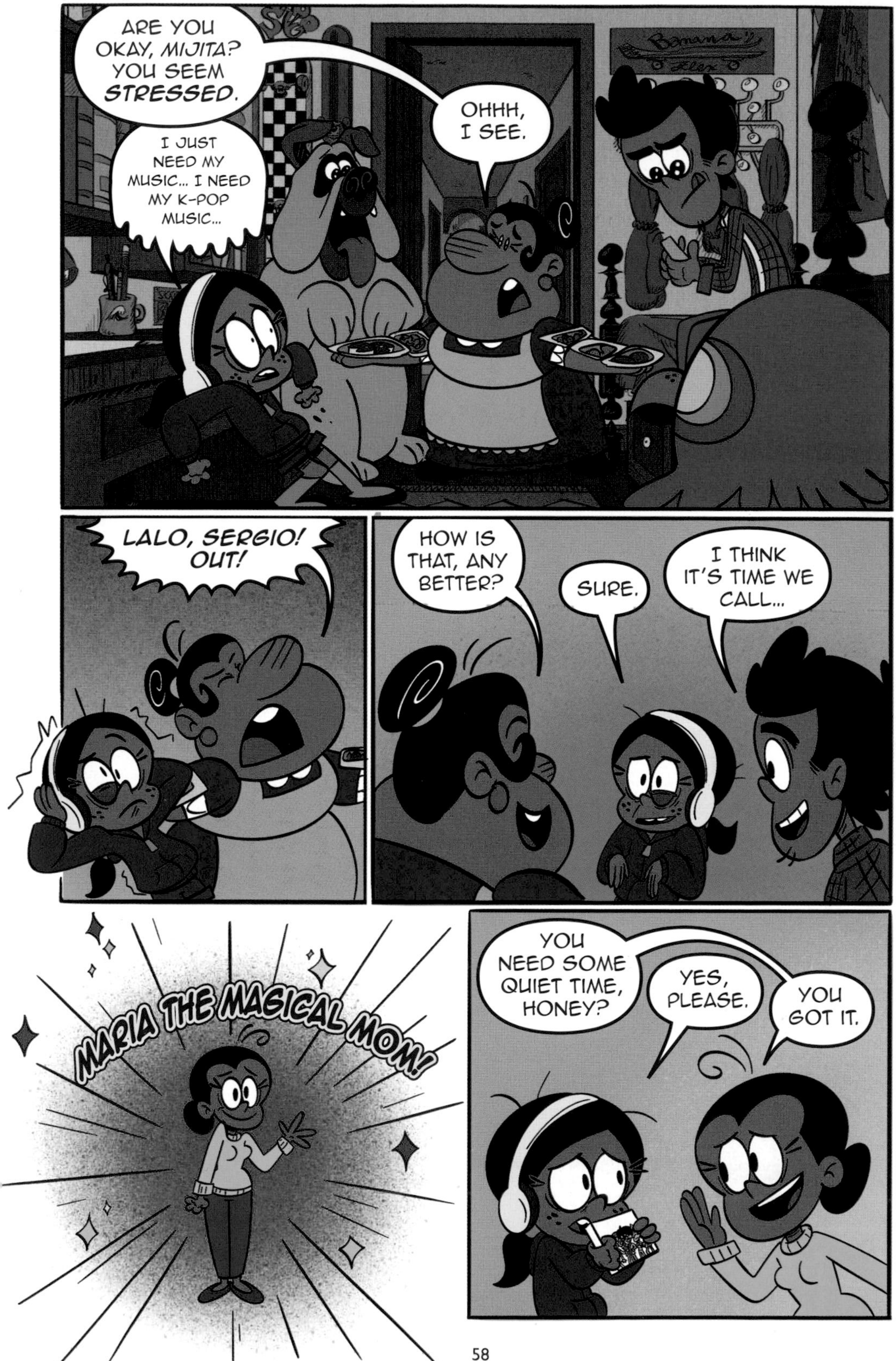
ARE YOU OKAY, MIJITA? YOU SEEM STRESSED.
I JUST NEED MY MUSIC... I NEED MY K-POP MUSIC...
OHHH, I SEE.
LALO, SERGIO! OUT!
HOW IS THAT, ANY BETTER?
SURE.
I THINK IT'S TIME WE CALL...
MARIA THE MAGICAL MOM!
YOU NEED SOME QUIET TIME, HONEY?
YES, PLEASE.
YOU GOT IT.

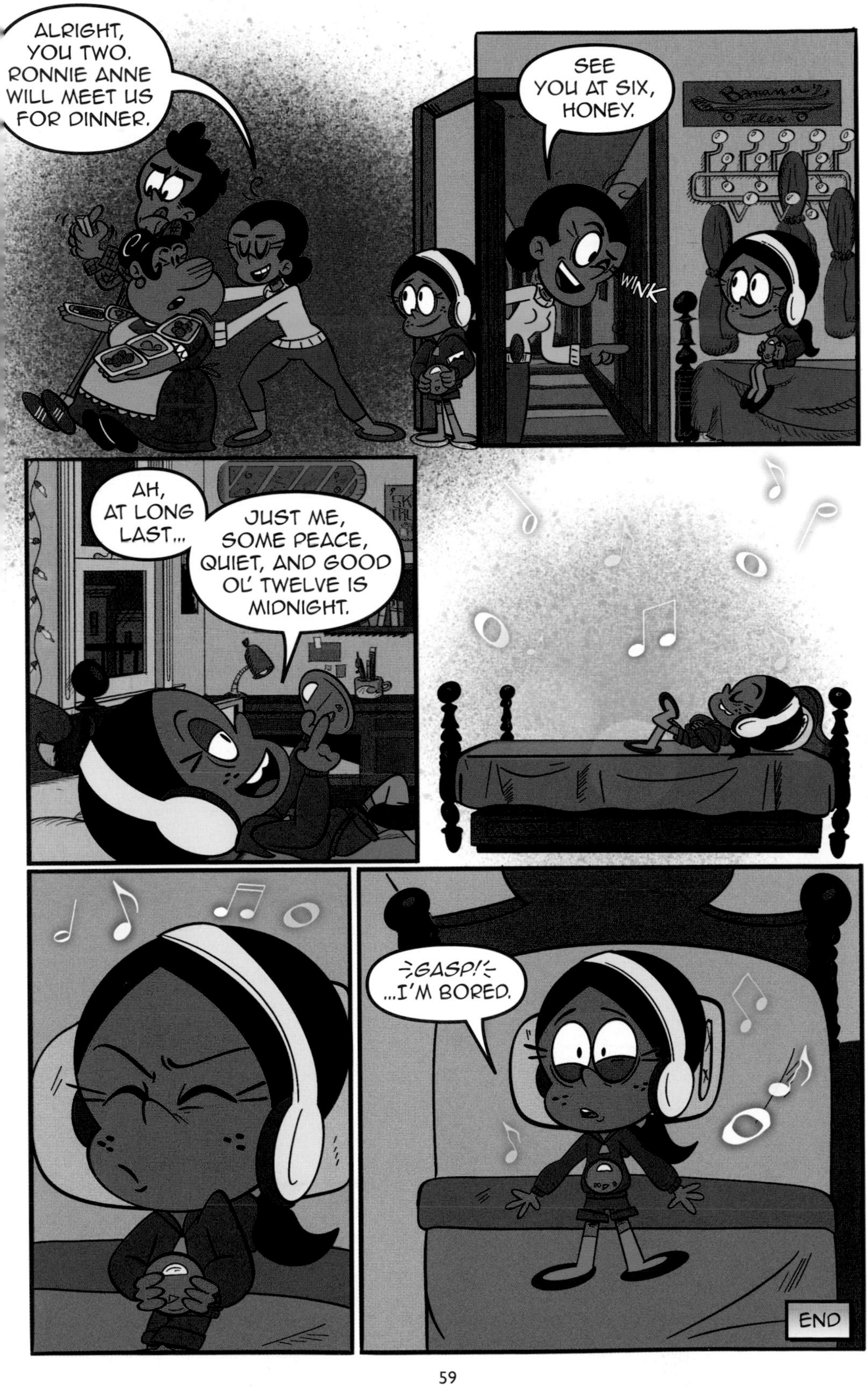
ALRIGHT, YOU TWO. RONNIE ANNE WILL MEET US FOR DINNER.
SEE YOU AT SIX, HONEY.
WINK
AH, AT LONG LAST...
JUST ME, SOME PEACE, QUIET, AND GOOD OL' TWELVE IS MIDNIGHT.
GASP! ...I'M BORED.
END

nickelodeon GRAPHIC NOVELS AVAILABLE FROM PAPERCUTZ

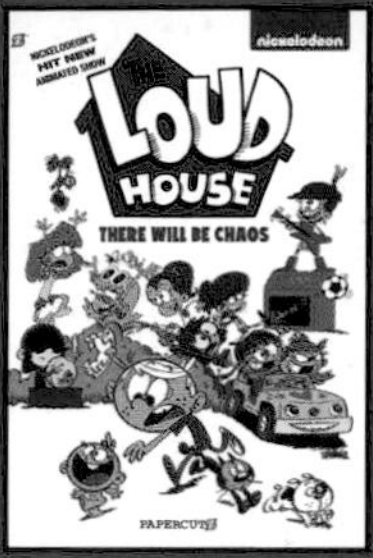
THE LOUD HOUSE
THERE WILL BE CHAOS
PAPERCUTZ

THE LOUD HOUSE
#1
"There Will Be Chaos"

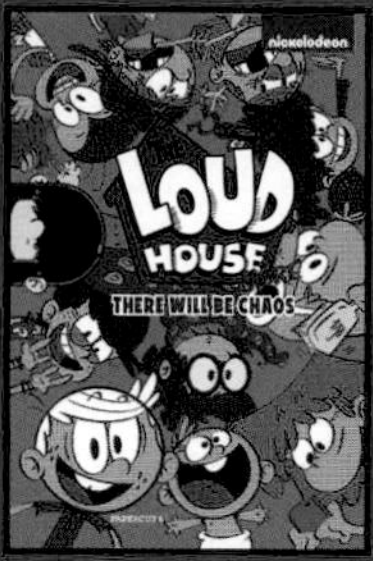
THE LOUD HOUSE
THERE WILL BE CHAOS

THE LOUD HOUSE
#2
"There Will Be More Chaos"

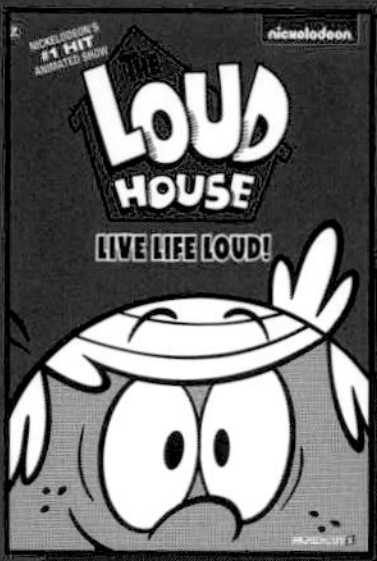
NICKELODEON'S #1 HIT ANIMATED SHOW
THE LOUD HOUSE
LIVE LIFE LOUD!

THE LOUD HOUSE
#3
"Live Life Loud!"

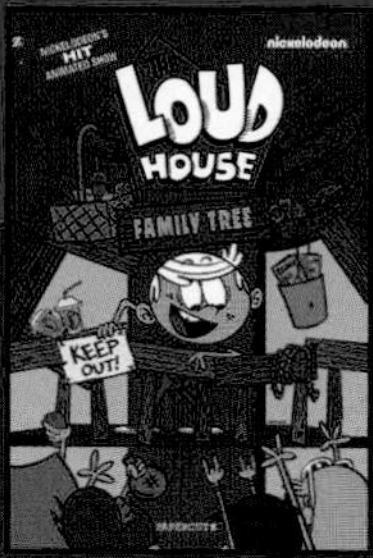
THE LOUD HOUSE
FAMILY TREE
KEEP OUT!

THE LOUD HOUSE
#4
"Family Tree"

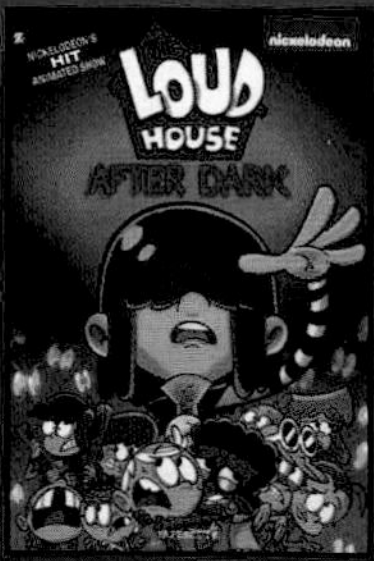
THE LOUD HOUSE
AFTER DARK

THE LOUD HOUSE
#5
"After Dark"

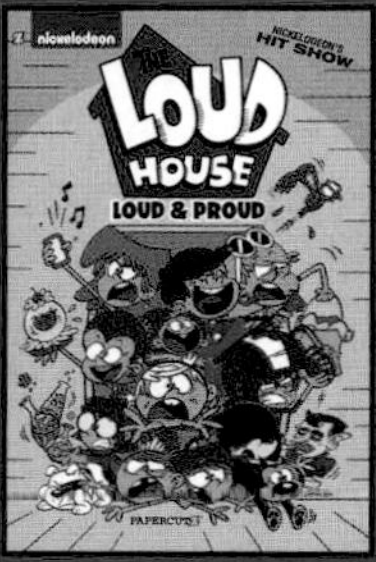
NICKELODEON'S HIT SHOW
THE LOUD HOUSE
LOUD & PROUD

THE LOUD HOUSE
#6
"Loud & Proud"

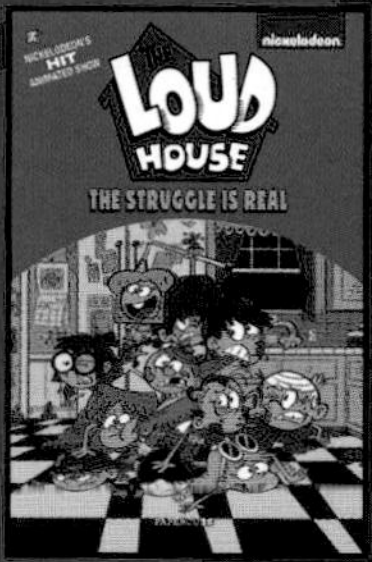
THE LOUD HOUSE
THE STRUGGLE IS REAL

THE LOUD HOUSE
#7
"The Struggle is Real"

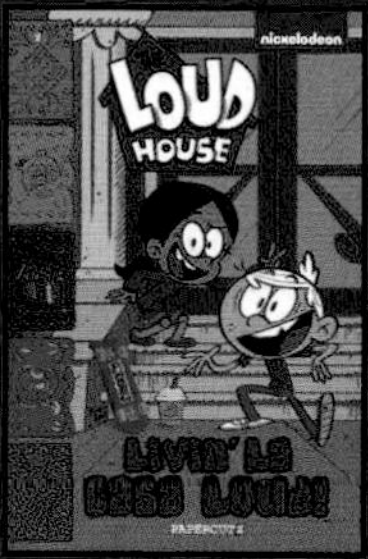
THE LOUD HOUSE
LIVIN' LA CASA LOUD!

THE LOUD HOUSE
#8
"Livin' La Casa Loud"

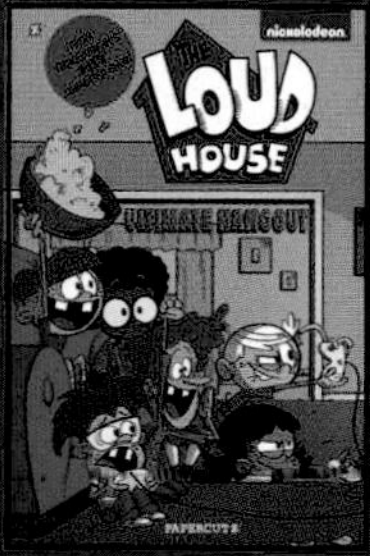
THE LOUD HOUSE
ULTIMATE HANGOUT

THE LOUD HOUSE
#9
"Ultimate Hangout"

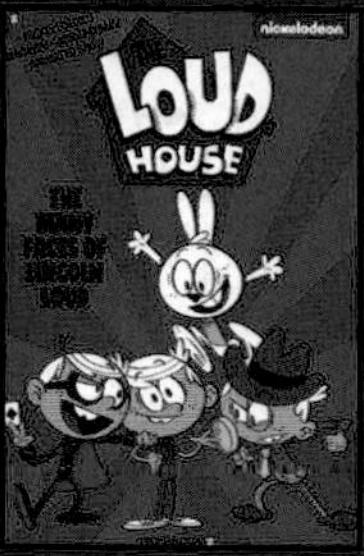
THE LOUD HOUSE
THE MANY FACES OF LINCOLN LOUD

THE LOUD HOUSE
#10
"The Many Faces of Lincoln Loud"

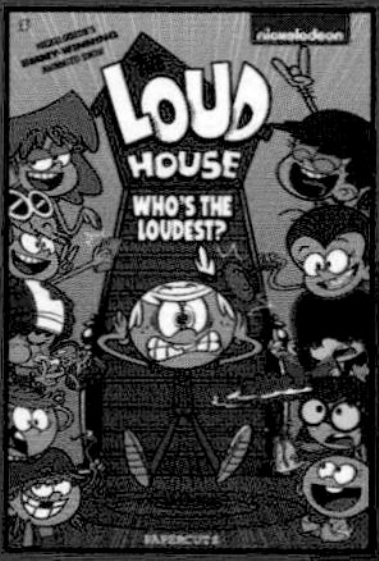
THE LOUD HOUSE
WHO'S THE LOUDEST?

THE LOUD HOUSE
#11
"Who's the Loudest?"

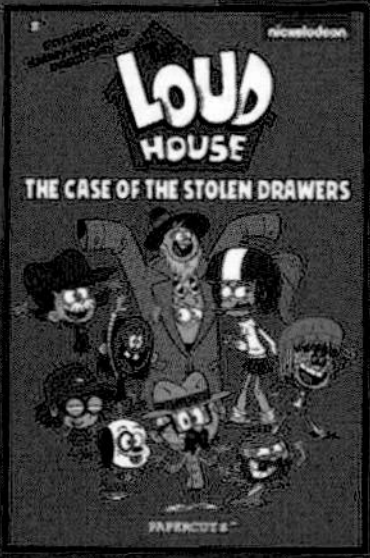
THE LOUD HOUSE
THE CASE OF THE STOLEN DRAWERS

THE LOUD HOUSE
#12
"The Case of the Stolen Drawers"

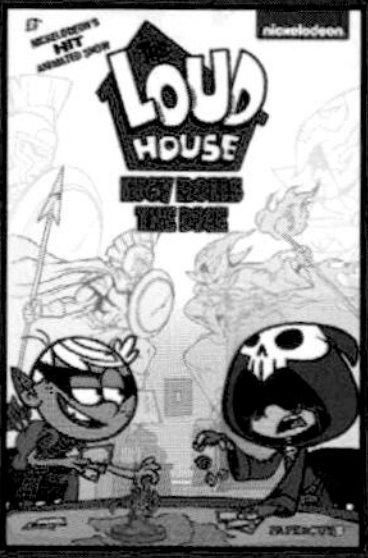
NICKELODEON'S HIT ANIMATED SHOW
THE LOUD HOUSE
LUCY ROLLS THE DICE

THE LOUD HOUSE
#13
"Lucy Rolls the Dice"

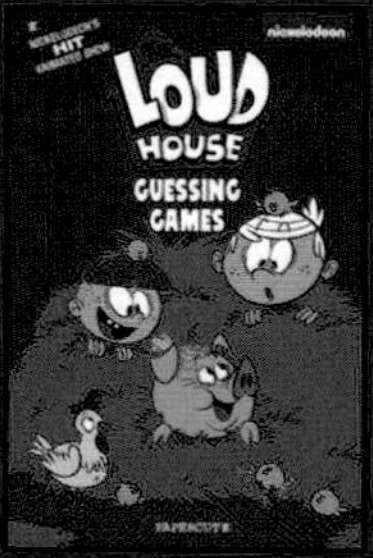
NICKELODEON'S HIT ANIMATED SHOW
THE LOUD HOUSE
GUESSING GAMES

THE LOUD HOUSE
#14
"Guessing Games"

COMING SOON

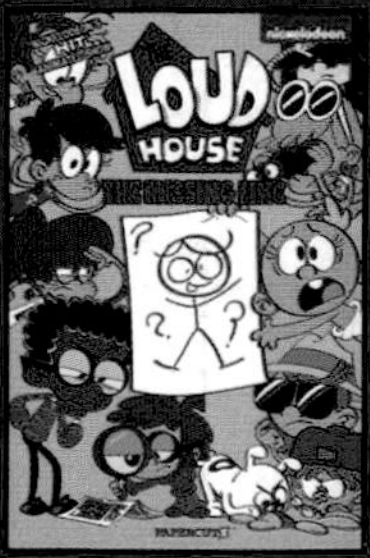
THE LOUD HOUSE
THE MISSING LINC

THE LOUD HOUSE
#15
"The Missing Linc"

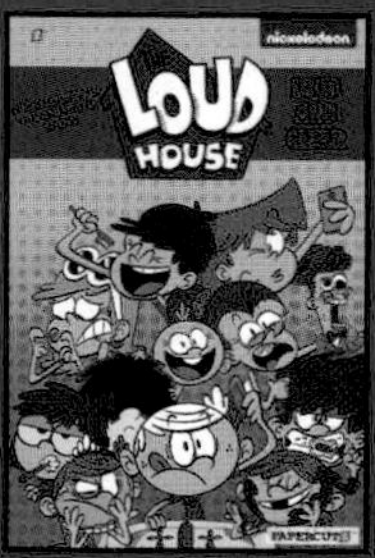
THE LOUD HOUSE

THE LOUD HOUSE
#16
"Loud and Clear"

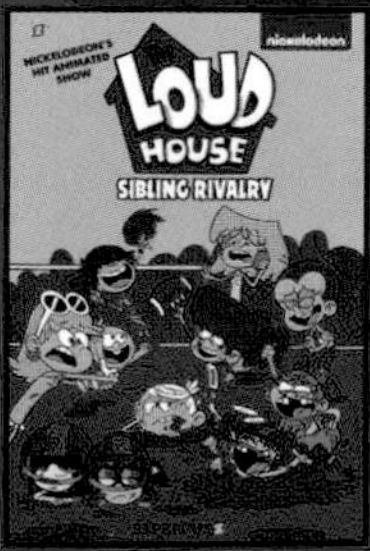
NICKELODEON'S HIT ANIMATED SHOW
THE LOUD HOUSE
SIBLING RIVALRY

THE LOUD HOUSE
#17
"Sibling Rivalry"

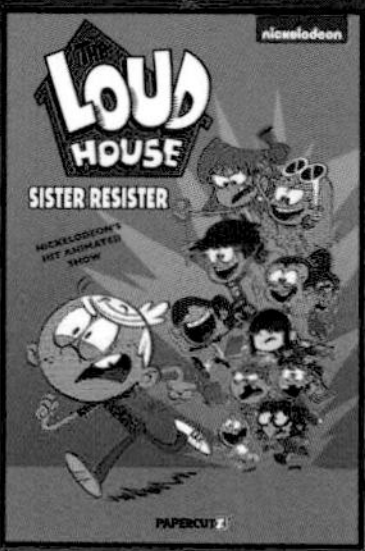
THE LOUD HOUSE
SISTER RESISTER
NICKELODEON'S HIT ANIMATED SHOW
PAPERCUTZ

THE LOUD HOUSE
#18
"Sister Resister"

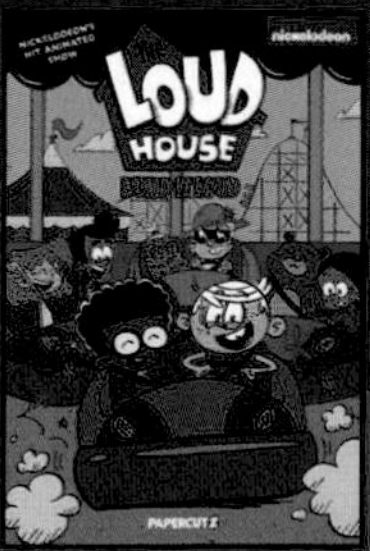
NICKELODEON'S HIT ANIMATED SHOW
THE LOUD HOUSE
PAPERCUTZ

THE LOUD HOUSE
#19
"Bump It Loud"

THE LOUD HOUSE
3 IN 1
#1

THE LOUD HOUSE
3 IN 1
#2

THE LOUD HOUSE
3 IN 1
#3

THE LOUD HOUSE
3 IN 1
#4

THE LOUD HOUSE
3 IN 1
#5

THE CASAGRANDES
#1
New Beginnings

THE CASAGRANDES
#2
Anything For Family

THE CASAGRANDES
#3
Brand Stinkin' New

THE CASAGRANDES
#4
Going Out of Business

THE CASAGRANDES
3 IN 1
#1

THE LOUD HOUSE
WINTER SPECIAL

THE LOUD HOUSE
SUMMER SPECIAL

THE LOUD HOUSE
LOVE OUT LOUD
SPECIAL

THE LOUD HOUSE
BACK TO SCHOOL
SPECIAL

THE LOUD HOUSE
SUPER SPECIAL

THE LOUD HOUSE
SPY SPECIAL

The Loud House and The Casagrandes graphic novels are also available digitally wherever e-books are sold.

Exclusive preview of THE LOUD HOUSE #19 "Bump It Loud"

"NOTHING BUT THE TOOTH"

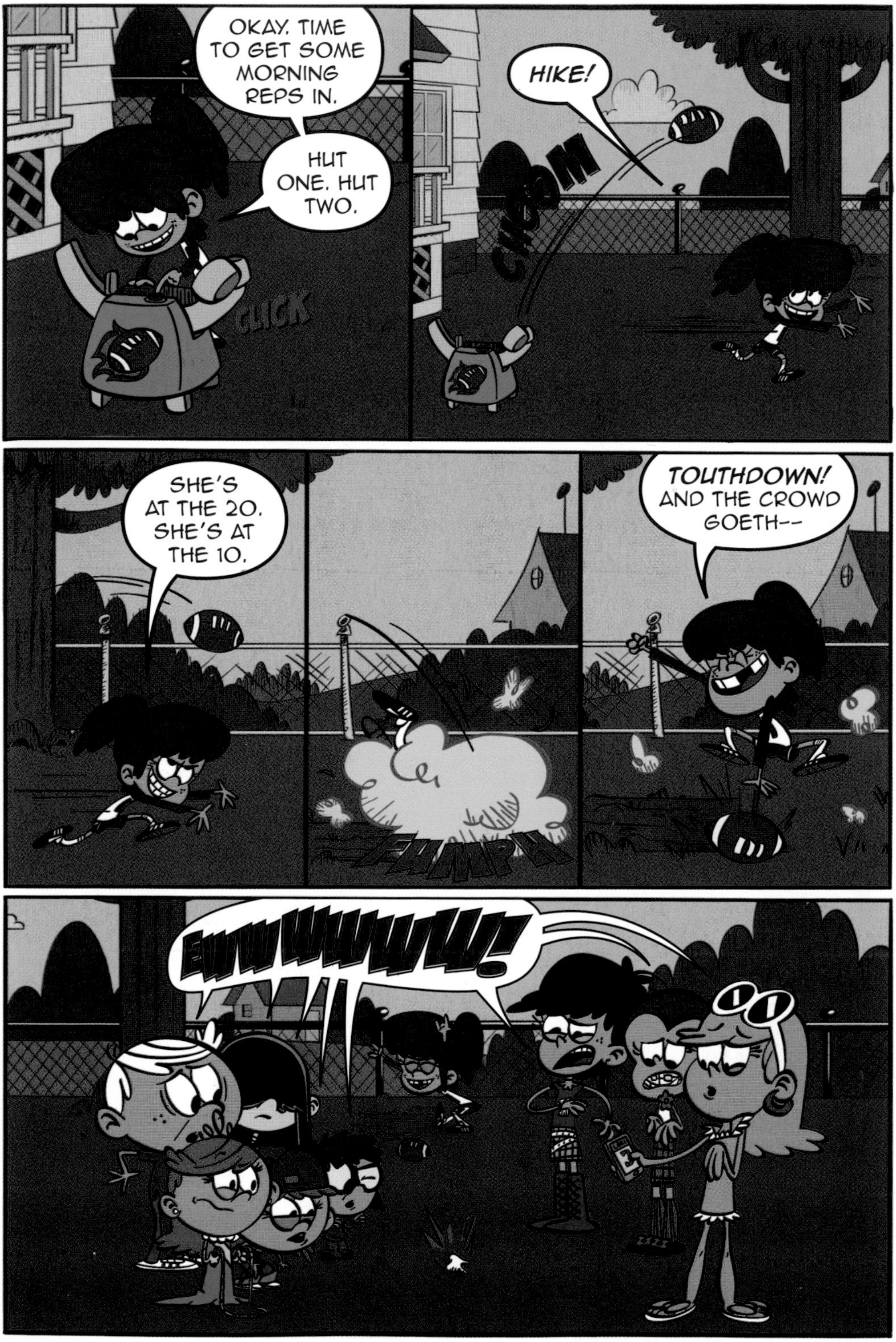
OKAY. TIME TO GET SOME MORNING REPS IN.
HUT ONE. HUT TWO.
CLICK
HIKE!
CHOOM
SHE'S AT THE 20. SHE'S AT THE 10.
FUMPH
TOUTHDOWN! AND THE CROWD GOETH--

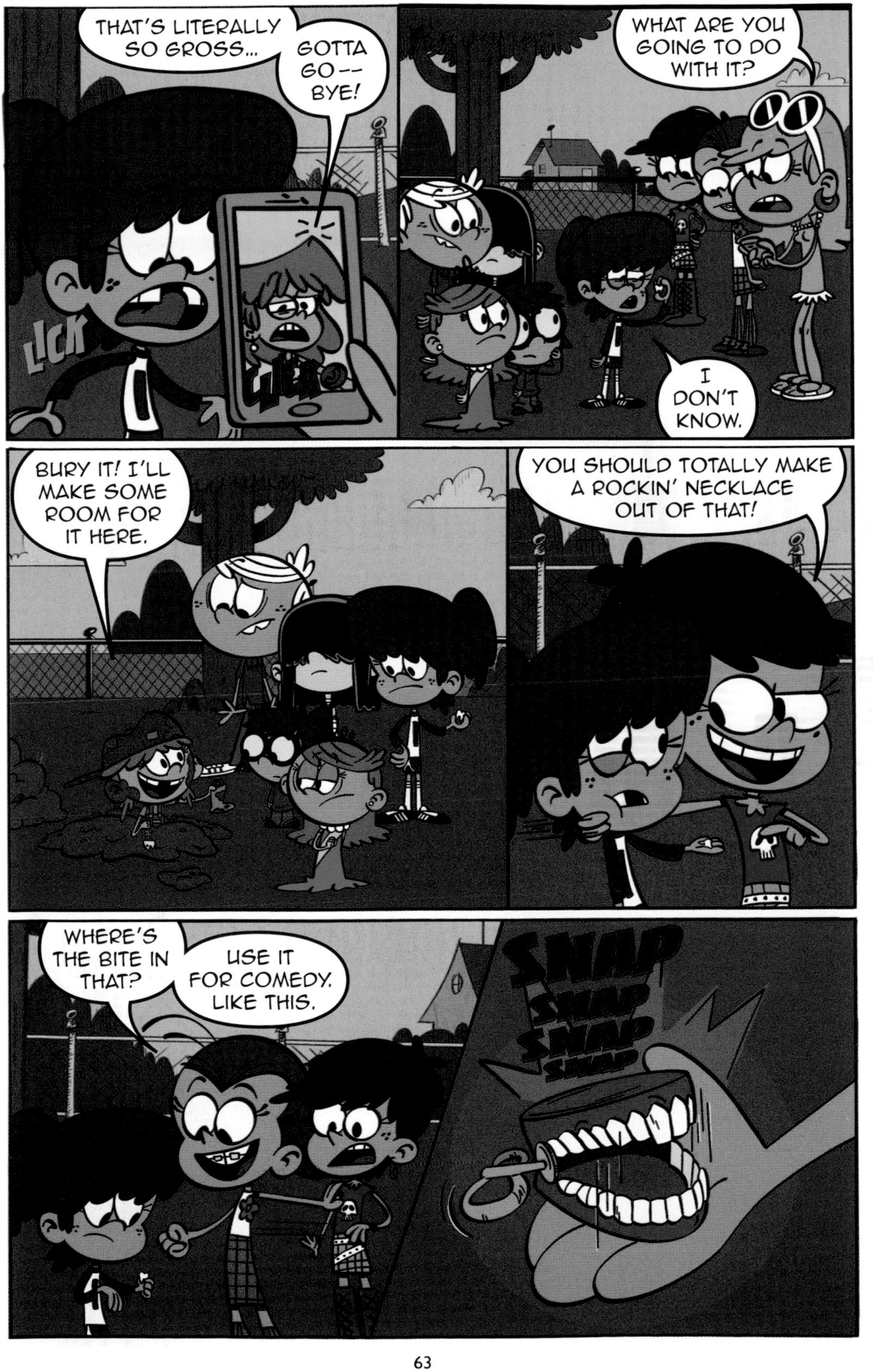
THAT'S LITERALLY SO GROSS...
GOTTA GO-- BYE!
LICK
WHAT ARE YOU GOING TO DO WITH IT?
I DON'T KNOW.
BURY IT! I'LL MAKE SOME ROOM FOR IT HERE.
YOU SHOULD TOTALLY MAKE A ROCKIN' NECKLACE OUT OF THAT!
WHERE'S THE BITE IN THAT?
USE IT FOR COMEDY. LIKE THIS.
SNAP
SNAP
SNAP
SNAP

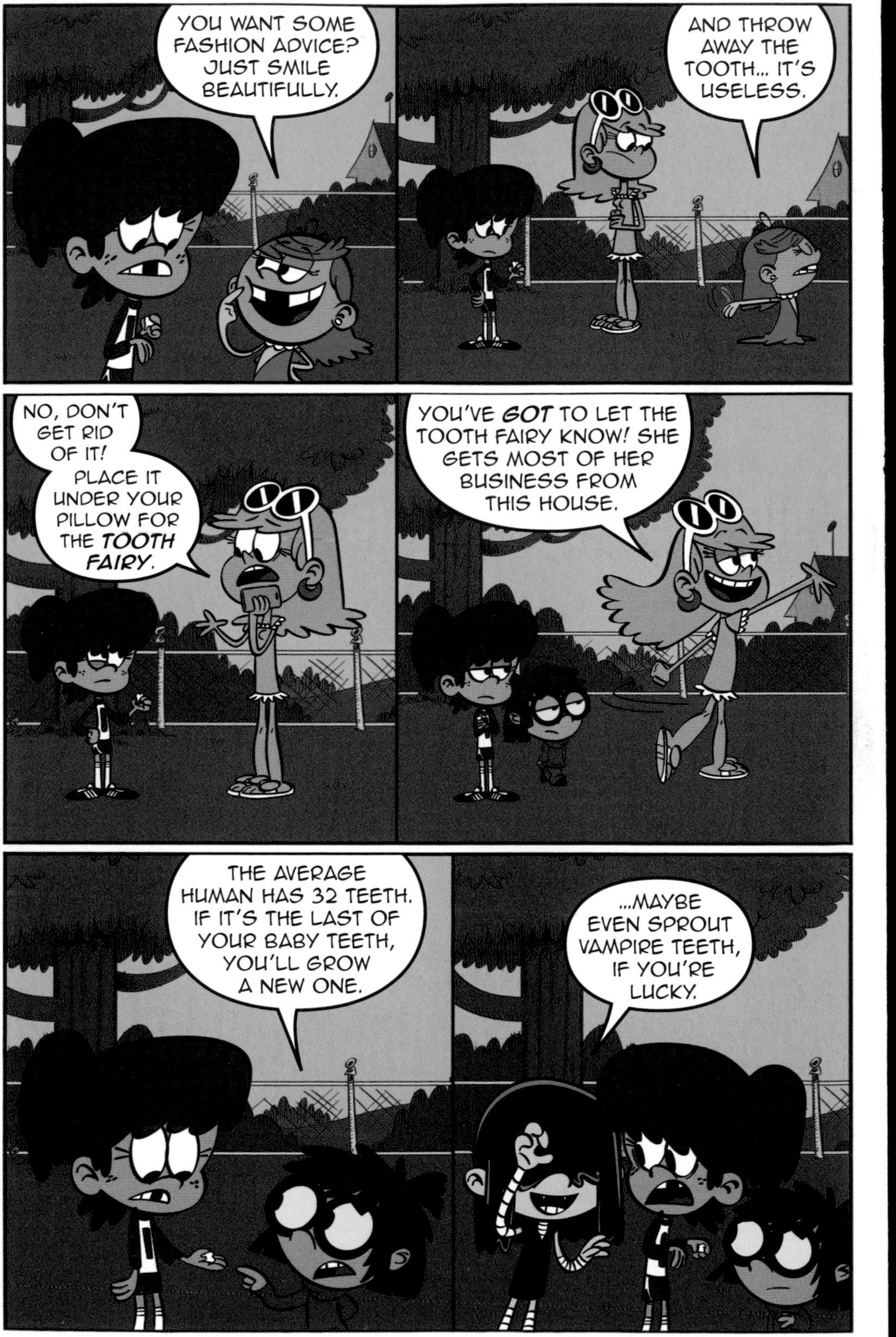

YOU WANT SOME FASHION ADVICE? JUST SMILE BEAUTIFULLY.
AND THROW AWAY THE TOOTH... IT'S USELESS.
NO, DON'T GET RID OF IT!
PLACE IT UNDER YOUR PILLOW FOR THE *TOOTH FAIRY*.
YOU'VE ***GOT*** TO LET THE TOOTH FAIRY KNOW! SHE GETS MOST OF HER BUSINESS FROM THIS HOUSE.
THE AVERAGE HUMAN HAS 32 TEETH. IF IT'S THE LAST OF YOUR BABY TEETH, YOU'LL GROW A NEW ONE.
...MAYBE EVEN SPROUT VAMPIRE TEETH, IF YOU'RE LUCKY.

THE LOUD HOUSE #19 will be available at your local libraries and booksellers soon!